CW01471996

SHERLOCK HOLMES

AND THE
MIDNIGHT BELL

David James

Ian Henry Publications

ISBN 0 86025 292 2

Published by
Ian Henry Publications, Ltd.
20 Park Drive, Romford, Essex RM1 4LH
and printed by
WBC Book Manufacturers, Ltd.
Waterton Industrial Estate, Bridgend, Glamorgan CF31 3XP

PREFACE

I am indebted to the beneficiaries of the will of the late John James Hudson for the provenance of the five stories which follow.

J. J. Hudson, who died two years ago at the age of eighty-six, was the grandson of the landlady and housekeeper of Mr. Sherlock Holmes and Doctor John H. Watson at 221B Baker Street.

When Mr. Sherlock Holmes left London for the little farm on the Sussex Downs, he presented Mrs. Hudson with a ledger containing several of his cases as a memento of his stay under her roof. There is an inscription to this effect, signed S. H., at the beginning of the manuscript.

When the estate of J. J. Hudson was wound up, soon after his death, this ledger was discovered.

The beneficiaries knew of my interest in the history of Mr. Sherlock Holmes, and allowed me to examine the ledger. I became convinced that it was genuine, saw that the cases were hitherto unknown, and managed to persuade them that they should be published.

David James
February, 2000

The Adventure of the Midnight Bell

It was a cold, rainy November afternoon, with a strong wind. Although it was only three, outside it was almost dark. An hour earlier, I had put on my oilskins and galoshes and gone out to buy a pound of strong pipe tobacco for Holmes. Even then the darkening sky had portended worse to come.

I could, of course, have sent down for the tobacco, but I had felt the need to get out of our rooms for a while, even in such inclement weather as this. Holmes had become increasingly irritable of late, nothing of any interest had occurred to engage his attention, and I had watched his slow descent into ennui.

He had been in a black mood for more than a week, and had spent most of that time lounging in an armchair, playing melancholy music on his violin, and, more than once, had sought comfort in his syringe and seven per cent solution.

His temper had not been improved by a letter he had received the day before. He had glanced at the letter, and with an oath, thrown it in the fire. I had been sitting opposite him, and had recovered it before it was burned. It was from the parish of Lampton, Sussex.

Dear Mr. Holmes, (it read)
I would like to consult you, if convenient, at four in the afternoon, on Tuesday the 16th of this month, about the strange behaviour of our church bell.
I am your obedient servant.
Charles Farthing (Rev.)

Tuesday the 16th was that day, and I anticipated his arrival with interest, not only because of my curiosity, but also for the sake of my companion's state of mind. When however, I had tried to discuss the letter with Holmes, he had been openly contemptuous. "I suppose he thinks that I have nothing better to do with my time than to chat to him about some trivial aberration of his bell," he expostulated.

"But you must see him, Holmes," I protested.

"Must I? Oh, I suppose I must," he said. "I certainly can't claim to be too busy, at any rate," he said, with a trace of bitterness.

At four precisely, Mrs. Hudson showed the clergyman up to our rooms. Holmes, despite his mood of the last week, had calmed down considerably. Secretly, I believed that he was pleased at the prospect of a break in the boredom of the foregoing days, however inconsequential it might turn out to be.

The reverend proved to be a tall, young man of slight build, evidently not long out of theological college. His face, reddened by the cold wind, bore a troubled and somewhat apologetic expression.

"I am extremely sorry to trouble you at such short notice, and on such a trivial matter," said he, "but I felt I had to come and see you. I have nobody else to turn to."

"It's quite all right," said Holmes with surprising courtesy, considering his reaction to the clergyman's letter. He held up his hand, as if to stem the tide of the clergyman's apologies. "Please come and sit down before the fire. You must be cold after your journey on such a day as this. When you have warmed yourself, I shall be glad to hear what you have to say. This, by the way, is my friend, Doctor Watson."

The vicar, who refused all offers of refreshment, made himself comfortable in front of the fire, and after we were all seated, he began his narrative.

"First of all, Mr. Holmes, you should know that I have not had this living very long - less than two years in fact. The parish is small, with just over one thousand souls. It was one of exceptional peace and tranquillity, I say 'was', because about two weeks ago, at midnight on a Sunday night, the church bell began to ring, seemingly of its own accord.

"Perhaps I should explain that we only have one bell, and we would not have even that, were it not for the kindness of the squire, who, soon after my arrival, paid for repairs to the belfry, and arranged for the purchase and instalment of a new bell. The old bell was cracked, and had been since the latter days of my predecessor. The ringing of it was the cause of rather more amusement than devotion and had become something of a joke."

"Yes, yes, I understand the position," said Holmes, with a touch of the irritation of the last few days. "You say the bell began to ring at midnight on a Sunday night?"

"And on two occasions since," said the vicar.

"Also at midnight?" asked Holmes.

"Yes, it rang at midnight on the other occasions," said the clergyman. "But the second time it rang was a Wednesday, the third a Friday."

"I presume you went to the church to investigate?"

"Yes, I got to the church within five minutes on the first and second occasions," said the reverend. "The church is only about fifty yards from the vicarage. The third time I had been waiting up for some days in readiness and, when I entered the church, the bell was still tolling. However, before I could reach the belfry, it had stopped."

"Did you see anyone?" asked Holmes.

"Alas! on each occasion the church and grounds were deserted," said the clergyman, with a slight shake of his head. "I should add that the church is never kept locked."

"It is certainly a curious phenomenon," mused Holmes. "Even if this is a prank, perpetrated by village youths, it does not explain how church and grounds were deserted each time."

"It has been suggested by some that there is a secret passage leading from the church to the squire's house," said the

3

vicar. "Both buildings date from the same era. The passage was said to have been constructed in the event that the house of the squire was besieged, during more troubled times than we enjoy now. I have made enquiries, but there is no evidence to support such a suggestion.

"I have also spoken to the squire, who says that he can vouch for everyone in his household, and that he has never heard of such a secret passage. His house is within earshot of the sound of the bell, it is less than half a mile away to the north, and he has made no secret of the fact that he also will wait in readiness until the next occasion and will keep his horse saddled, so that he can come to my aid as soon as he hears the bell. He has also said that he will give the culprit, or culprits, a severe thrashing if he gets his hands on them. A course of action that I cannot, as a man of God, endorse. He is a good man, but he is subject to fits of ungovernable rage."

Holmes settled back in his chair, a dreamy expression upon his face, the tension of the past few days had left him, and I could tell that the clergyman's story interested him exceedingly.

"I shall be glad to look into your case," said Holmes. "But until or unless there are further developments, I am afraid that I cannot spare the time to come down to your parish."

"I am glad you have seen fit to take this case," said Mr Farthing, with relief showing in his face. "It means a lot to me and my parishioners."

"Have you had the misfortune to quarrel with anyone in your parish in the last few weeks?" asked Holmes.

The clergyman looked uncomfortable. "Yes. I had words with the sexton, Edwards, about a month ago on the matter of employment of gravediggers, but it was really nothing serious."

"What can you tell me about Edwards?" asked Holmes.

"Well, there is not much to tell," said the reverend. "He has been the sexton at Lampton for many years, before even my predecessor's time, and is a man who is somewhat quiet and reserved. He is about sixty years old, frail, but in good health and active. He lives alone, and as far as I know he has never been married. In recent years he has been unable to dig the graves himself, and his been forced to use some men from the village for that purpose. It was on account of this that we had our disagreement: I felt that he should give up his post to a younger man, but he would not hear of it."

"One last question, Mr Farthing," said Holmes. "Have you formed any opinions, or drawn any conclusions, from these singular incidents?"

"I cannot say that I have," replied he. "I cannot think of anyone who would wish to do such a thing, and the manner of its accomplishment is a mystery to me."

The minister rose to leave, thanked Holmes and I again for looking into the case, and promised to let us know of any further incidents.

After the clergyman had gone, Holmes spent a little time looking him up in *Crockford's*. He closed the book with a snap, and then sat in front of the fire, puffing on his oldest and blackest pipe. Outside, the weather had doubled its fury, the wind moaned in the chimney, and the rain lashed the windows. I sat opposite, reading one of the yellow-backed novels which had oft been the source of my friend's derision, by the light of a flickering candle. Holmes took the pipe from his lips and broke the silence.

"I don't like it, Watson," he declared. "I shall be very surprised if we don't hear something from our reverend friend very soon.

The next day brought no news, nor the next, but on the Friday morning, a wire arrived. On reading it, my friend frowned and gave an exclamation of dismay. He handed it to me without a word.

5

Come at once. There has been a double disaster. (it read)
Charles Farthing.

"I was afraid of this, Watson," muttered Holmes, as he hurriedly got ready to leave. "But what could I do?"

I made some expression of sympathy.

"If you would look up the times of the trains to Lampton, I would be very much obliged to you," said Holmes.

There happened to be a train within the hour, and soon Holmes and I were ensconced in a carriage on our way to Lampton. The bad weather of Tuesday had given way to a cold, dry, windless day, with occasional glimpses of a watery sun.

It was a good thing that our journey was comparatively short, because my friend sat opposite me with ill-concealed impatience.

He had had time to send a wire to the vicar from Victoria, telling him which train to meet and on arrival at Lampton, the vicar was there to meet us, in a very agitated state.

"Mr. Holmes, Mr. Holmes," he said, wringing his hands. "I'm so very glad to see you! The squire has been murdered, and the sexton has gone missing. The police have issued a warrant for his arrest."

When we arrived at the vicarage, there were a number of carriages in the drive, each bearing the legend: SUSSEX POLICE. And there seemed be at least a dozen officers examining every inch of the church grounds, and surrounding area.

We were shown into the vicar's study, where we found the vicar's wife, a uniformed sergeant, and a short, well-built, dark-haired man of about forty, who introduced himself to us as Inspector Pringle.

"I am delighted to have you here, Mr. Holmes," he said. "But I think you have had a wasted journey, for when we catch the sexton, I think that will be the end of the matter."

6

"We shall see," said Holmes, "and now I would be glad if the vicar could give us an account of the recent events."

"At a few minutes past midnight last night," said the clergyman, obviously still shaken and distressed, "the bell began to ring, as before. I was already up and dressed and reached the church within a few minutes, but again I could find no-one in the church or grounds. I was on my way back to the vicarage, when I heard a terrible scream, it seemed to come from a small clump of trees, about half-way between here and the squire's house on the hill. The lane which leads from the house to the village runs through the middle of the trees.

"I had my lantern with me, and started up the lane, the entrance being a matter of about one hundred yards down the road which runs past the vicarage, with all haste, towards the clump of trees. Near the foot of the hill, in the same lane, is the sexton's house. The door of the house was ajar, and there was a light in the window, I knocked at the door, and even looked around inside, but he was not there, and in the end I went on alone. Just before I reached the trees, I came upon the squire's horse, grazing at the side of the lane. When I reached the point in the lane where it passes through the trees, I found the body of the squire."

At this point the vicar lapsed into silence, and the account was taken up by the Inspector.

"He found the body of the squire. He had died from severe injuries to his head. If it was not for the fact that the sexton has gone missing, it is possible that his death would have been put down to a tragic mishap."

Holmes gave a little start at this, which I alone noticed, but otherwise remained impassive.

"I think our reverend friend would do well to go and lie down for a while," said Holmes. "Perhaps there is something in your bag that you can give him, Watson."

7

The vicar was prevailed upon to lie down and, after I had given him a sedative, I left him in the care of his wife.

Holmes, the Inspector, and I, then set out for the spot where the squire's body had been found.

Near the bottom of the lane, the Inspector pointed out the house of the missing sexton. He also told us that the sexton's bed had not been slept in on the previous night. We entered the house, outside which a constable stood on guard. In the kitchen, on a scrubbed pine table, stood a half-eaten, simple meal of bread and cheese, also a full cup of tea. It was obvious that the sexton had been at his supper when he had felt compelled to go out. We left the house, and continued on our way.

A short walk up the narrow lane, which was unpaved and rutted, brought us to the murder scene. Here the lane was at a much lower level than the surrounding fields and trees, it had been cut through a slight rise in the ground, and rain and the passage of traffic had further reduced its level, so that at this point, it resembled the dry bed of a deep stream. At the sides of the lane were a number of large stones, which had been exposed by this same weathering, and had been moved to one side at some time, to allow the passage of carriages and other wheeled vehicles. A few curious onlookers were gathered just before the trees, and were being kept back by a constable. The Inspector dispersed them by curtly telling them that there was nothing to see, and that they should go about their business.

In the centre of the lane, at the murder scene, was a large stone, considerably bloodstained. The body had been removed, the Inspector told us, to the squire's house. He told us that the squire had been found lying in the lane, with his head on the stone. Holmes scrutinised the object carefully, lifted it briefly, and dropped it back. He then rolled it over to examine its underside. Holmes seemed to gather momentum after this, he darted around, examining the sides of the lane, the trees growing nearby, and the thick bushes which grew beneath the trees on both sides of the lane. He first explored the bushes on the church side, and then the bushes on the other side. Suddenly he gave a low whistle, as of someone making a discovery and called to us to join him - when we did, we could see that he had found a length of thin, but strong, tarred rope, tied close to the base of a tree and half hidden in the shrubbery.

"My sergeant found that, but we assumed that it had been used to tether an animal at some time," said the Inspector.

"No," said Holmes. "This rope was instrumental in the murder of the squire. See how there was a loop at the other end, which has been cut through, not at the first attempt, nor the second, but on the third. Next to the cut are two knife slashes which failed to sever it."

Next, Holmes took the free end of the rope, and, crossing to the other side of the lane with it, he found a tree which fitted the cut loop, the rope now being tightly stretched.

"This tree bears traces of the tarry matter with which the rope is impregnated," said Holmes, "and when the cut loop is wrapped around the tree, scratches on the bark of the tree correspond to the cuts made in the rope. There is no doubt in my mind that this rope has been tied to these two trees, so that it was tightly stretched across the lane, at such a height that someone on horseback, especially someone in haste, as the squire must have been, would have come into contact with the rope and been dismounted by it. On a night when the moon was in its first quarter, as was the case last night, it would have been almost impossible to see. It is obvious that the person who cut the rope, in the way I have described, was the murderer."

"Why didn't the murderer remove the rope altogether, Holmes?" I asked.

"It was the intention of the murderer to remove the rope after the crime had been completed," said Holmes. "But there is evidence to show that before he could do so, he was surprised by the arrival of a third party."

"All this is going too fast for me," cried the Inspector.

"Before you came we were all looking for the sexton, and now you say that three people took part in this tragedy."

"Perhaps it would be easier for everyone," said Holmes. If I were to reconstruct the crime. This then is what occurred: The murderer waited until all was dark and quiet, then he tied the rope across the lane. He had previously selected a large and heavy stone, which, by the way, must be at least forty pounds in weight. He removed the stone from the side of the lane, you can see the depression in the ground where it had previously rested - the earth there is still damp, and placed it near the end of the rope, in the bushes on the church side of the lane, in a position of readiness. I now come to a part of the reconstruction which I think you will find hard to accept. The murderer, in some way upon which I hope to throw light very soon, caused the church bell to ring."

The Inspector tutted at this and shook his head.

"Yes, I know, Inspector, it is incredible," said Holmes, "but I can assure you that it was so. After he rang the bell, he hastened back to this spot to await the arrival of the squire. He knew the squire would come, because he had heard what was, by then, common knowledge in the village: that the squire intended to ride down to the church on the next occasion the bell was rung, to give the perpetrators a sound thrashing, and that he kept a horse saddled in readiness for this purpose.

"When the squire was thrown off his horse by the rope, the murderer picked up the stone and dashed it down on his head, while he was still on the ground after his fall. After he did so, he started to cover his tracks. It had always been the intention of the murderer to make the whole thing seem like a tragic accident. He had time to remove the stone from the squire's head and, instead, arranged it so that the unfortunate man's head lay upon it. I have examined the stone and there is blood and hair on the side next to the ground when we arrived, as well as a large amount of blood on the surface upper-most at that time. It was after he had arranged the body in this way, that he heard, or saw, someone coming to investigate the scream made by the squire at the moment that the rope unhorsed him. This third party may have carried a light, which the murderer would have seen. I do not think that the squire could have screamed after the stone hit his head, he would have been killed instantly.

"The murderer, slashed frantically at the rope on the church side, but only managed to sever it at the third attempt, this was a measure of his agitation at that time. When he did cut through it, he only had time to fling it across the lane, where it was discovered later, and make his getaway."

"And who was this third party you keep referring to?" said the Inspector drily. "The vicar I suppose."

"No," said Holmes. "The third party was almost certainly the sexton. His house was the nearest to this spot, and, because he had quarrelled with the vicar fairly recently, he had almost certainly decided to conduct his own investigation into the mysterious, nocturnal bell-ringing, without taking him into his confidence. It is my belief that he too, was keeping a vigil at night, and this enabled him to be the first at the murder scene."

"If what you say is true," said the Inspector, "where is the sexton now, eh? Answer me that."

"I don't think it will be long before we find the sexton," replied Holmes. "I believe he is not far from here."

"If, as you say, he is not far from here," rejoined the Inspector. "Why does he not come forward to throw some light on these mysterious events?"

"I said he is not far from here," said Holmes. "I did not say that he is still alive."

"What! You don't mean to tell me that he too has been murdered," retorted the Inspector, unable to keep his mounting incredulity in check.

"Yes," said Holmes. "I think he too has been slain. I believe he went in pursuit of the murderer of the squire, and was over-powered and killed by him. You must realise that, when the murderer was disturbed, he became a desperate man with all his plans in disarray. Also, Inspector, consider this: could the sexton, a frail old man, lift a stone of that weight and use it as a weapon in the way I have described?"

Some of the doubt and disbelief left the Inspector's face at this, and he became more pensive. "Well, gentlemen," said the Inspector at last. "I think I will leave you to your own devices, to pursue my inquiries in the village."

With that he departed, leaving Holmes and I with the bemused constable.

"I think, Watson," said Holmes. "That it is a splendid day for a little walk in the country." Holmes climbed up the slope on the church side of the lane, and disappeared into the shrubbery, and I followed him as best I could.

Our walk took us through the bushes, and over a crude fence into a field where a few sheep grazed, this field sloped quite steeply in the direction of the church. Holmes and I made our way down to the bottom of the field, it was only a matter of a couple of hundred yards. At this point was another fence, and just beyond that a sharp declivity, which ended at the level of the grounds at the rear of the church, and afforded an excellent view of those grounds and the vicarage. A few constables were sitting in the churchyard, having a quiet smoke.

Probably stone from this part of the hillside had been used to build the church and vicarage, as well as other houses and buildings in the village. Therefore the church and vicarage lay in a u-shaped hollow, as if some giant had taken a bite out the hill. Holmes and I now stood at a point almost level with the top of the belfry, this was situated at the rear of the church, and less than a hundred feet away. Holmes now threw himself into a minute examination of the land, between the fence and the edge of the man-made cliff, where a few bushes grew. When he had finished his face was dark with vexation.

"Those constables have been up here," he said, "and they have trampled on every inch of the ground. There is nothing to be gained from staying up here now, Watson, we will better employ our time by investigating the belfry. There is, however, one more thing we can do while we are here, we can find out how long it takes to get back to the murder scene."

With this Holmes took out his watch, and we retraced our steps, as quickly as we could, back up the field to the clump of trees where the unfortunate squire had met his end.

"I make it just over two minutes," said Holmes, as we found ourselves once more next to the tree in the bushes, which had had the rope tied around it.

"I think," said Holmes, "that the murderer would have had ample time to ring the bell, and be back here for the squire's arrival."

"Doubtless," said I, "but how did the murderer ring the bell?"

"All in good time, Watson," said he. "All in good time."

Together, we made our way back down the lane to the road leading to the church grounds.

Here, we once again encountered the Inspector, who seemed to be a lot less hostile than he was at our last meeting: he greeted us with something which approached geniality.

"Ah, Mr. Holmes and Doctor Watson," said he, "and how is your investigation proceeding?"

"I hope to have some results for you very soon, Inspector," said Holmes. "We are on our way to the top of the belfry."

"We have already been up there," said the Inspector "and have found nothing."

"I take it that you have no objection, in that case, to Watson and I having a look around up there?"

"You are welcome, Mr. Holmes," said he. "You will forgive me if I do not accompany you."

Holmes and I set out for the church, and, when we were out of earshot of the Inspector, Holmes surprised me by breaking into laughter - laughter which he muffled with his hand.

"What is so amusing, Holmes?" I asked.

"That Inspector!" said he. "He still has no faith in me or my methods, but has obviously decided to humour us, for the time being at least."

The ascent to the belfry was by means of a series of steep, somewhat rickety ladders, which we climbed with some difficulty. In the gloom of the belfry, the only light came from slits cut here and there in the stonework. Finally we came to the small room at the top of the belfry, on all four sides of which were openings with stone slats, and in the light which streamed through these we were able to see a little better.

The bell, although new, was already coated with a thin film of verdigris, and dust, and the floor was covered with a considerable layer of debris.

Holmes turned his attentions to the bell first, he gave particular scrutiny to the spoked, cast-iron pulley wheel which bore the bell-rope, he examined the spokes carefully, and at one point, placed his face close to the pulley wheel and sniffed deeply.

He then turned his attentions to the slatted opening which looked out towards the top of the declivity from which we had observed the church and grounds.

"See, Watson," he cried, pointing to a number of dark lines upon one of the slats "these are marks made by the same kind of rope which was tied across the lane, if you sniff them you will find that tarry smell. The same can be said of the spokes of the bell pulley."

I did as I was asked, and I could indeed detect a tarry smell around the pulley wheel and the stone slats.

"I think the manner in which the bell was rung on all those midnight occasions is obvious now," said he. "The murderer had only to bring his rope up into the belfry when everything was quiet - the view from that cliff would have helped him to judge when the moment was right. He then threaded the rope through the pulley wheel, and fed it through the slatted opening so that it hung down outside. He would already have let a rope down from the cliff at the rear of the church, and, on going outside, would have tied the rope from the belfry to the end of it, this he could easily accomplish before the midnight bell-ringing was to begin. He would then make his way to the top of the cliff, draw up his improvised bell-rope, and, when midnight approached, begin to ring the bell without fear of discovery."

"But surely," said I, "the rope tied to the pulley wheel would be seen the next day, the murderer would not dare to try and recover it after a night when he had roused the whole village."

"Ah," said Holmes, "he arranged to use a doubled-up rope, so that it was not tied to the pulley wheel, but only threaded through it. After he had finished ringing the bell, he only had to release one end of the doubled rope, and recover it, before anyone approached, by hauling on the other end."

Holmes and I descended from the belfry, and made our way out of the church.

"I think, Watson," said Holmes, "that we can best pass the next hour or so by having something to eat and drink at the local inn."

And so we shortly found ourselves at table in the inn. Holmes ate a hearty meal, for which I was profoundly glad, because he had only picked at his food during his inactivity of the previous ten days or so. After we had finished our repast, we sat in silence, Holmes deep in thought, smoking his pipe, and I looking out of the window which gave a view of the church in the distance.

After some time had passed in this way, I perceived a constable running down the road towards the inn. The man soon entered the room where we were sitting. "I was told that I would find you here," he gasped, out of breath. "We have found the body of the sexton."

We left the inn, and followed the constable up the road which led to the church, and back up the lane which led to the squire's house. When we got to the murder scene, we were met by the Inspector.

"I'm afraid I owe you an apology, Mr. Holmes," said he. "You have been right all along and we have been wrong. Now, if you would be so good as to follow me."

The Inspector, accompanied by two constables, one of whom was a local man who had known the sexton well, led us through the bushes into the field above the church once more. This time, however, our way led up the hill towards a thicket, beyond the fence at the top of the field. In the middle of the thicket, surrounded by bracken, brown and dry with the onset of winter, was a shaft about ten feet deep, like an half-choked mine shaft or well, a ladder was in place in it. When Holmes and I peered into it, we could see the body of a man. Next to it lay a lantern.

"We had searched in this thicket before," said the Inspector, "but the body was concealed by a considerable amount of bracken, which had been thrown down on top of it. I instructed two of my men to fetch a ladder, so that we could make a more thorough examination of this shaft, and that was when we discovered it."

"When your men first entered this thicket," asked Holmes, "was there any sign of a struggle?"

"No, Mr. Holmes, there was not," answered the Inspector. "That was another reason we did not inspect the shaft more closely at first."

Holmes went down the ladder, to look more closely at the body. Even from where I stood, I could see bruising around the unfortunate man's neck, which told more plainly than words how he had met his end. Holmes, at the bottom of the shaft, turned the body over and gave an exclamation. Tightly clutched in the dead man's hand, which had been under the body, was a large, brass key. Holmes took possession of this, and rejoined us at the top of the shaft.

"This key has been burnished by constant use," said Holmes. "Clearly also, it fits a large lock. A large lock means a large door, and therefore a large building. If this key is not found to be one which belonged to the sexton, it must prove, if you will forgive the bad play on words, to be one of the keys which will lead to the solution of these crimes."

The Inspector took the key, and placed it in his pocket. "I shall show this to the vicar, when he has recovered sufficiently," he said. "In the meantime we can try it in all the locks that the sexton had access to."

Holmes, the Inspector and I, walked back down the lane to the sexton's house, where we quickly established that the key did not fit any of his locks. When we got back to the churchyard, we found that it did not fit the locks of any of the buildings there, including those of the vicarage.

"The key almost certainly belongs to the murderer," said the Inspector, as we sat once more in the vicar's study, the vicar himself being still absent. "The sexton must have seized hold of it during his struggle with him, and in his haste to get away, he did not discover his loss."

"We are in a position now to put together a few facts about the murderer," said Holmes. "He is obviously a strongly-built man, cunning, and also young and active. It is obvious that he has a great deal of local knowledge also, and therefore he must be a local man. He must have planned to murder the squire for some time, and probably chose this method in order to make his death look like an accident. He hit on the idea of ringing the church bell - I will describe to you how he accomplished it later - to lure the squire to his death. He counted on the squire's irascible nature for this. He knew that the squire would, sooner or later, become involved in an attempt to clear up the mystery, especially since he, the squire, paid for the bell in the first place, and would have a proprietorial attitude towards it."

"It was a well known fact," said the Inspector. "That the squire disdained the use of his carriages, he preferred to ride on horseback wherever he went, regardless of the weather. He was not very well liked in the environs of the village, and had made many enemies, his wife among them. On one occasion they had a dreadful quarrel, and he threw her into his lily pond. In fact, about the only person in the village who had a good word to say about him was the vicar himself."

"The vicar had not been long in the village," I remarked. "Also, because of the squire's generosity in the matter of the new bell, he was inclined to look upon him favourably."

"What do you recommend as a course of action now, Mr. Holmes?" asked the Inspector.

"In the first place, we must keep the discovery of the key secret," said my friend. "It is possible that, when the murderer discovers his loss, he will come looking for it under cover of darkness. I doubt that he will try this, as it is my belief that we are dealing with a man too clever to be caught in that way, however, it might be worth leaving a few of your men behind tonight to keep watch on the general area of the murder scene."

"I will certainly do that," replied the Inspector.

"What can you tell me about the squire's wife, Inspector?" asked Holmes.

"She is young, twenty-five years of age, and pretty. She is about fifteen years younger than her late husband and is his second wife. His first wife died giving birth to their only child, there is no issue of the second marriage. She is a local woman, remembered as being a lively and outgoing person at the time of her marriage, which took place some four years ago. The villagers say that a dramatic change took place in her soon after marriage: she became sullen and withdrawn, especially since the incident of the lily pond. That is all I can tell you."

"When did the business of the lily pond take place?" asked Holmes.

"About a year ago," replied the Inspector.

"Thank you, Inspector, I think I have found out all I need to know."

At this point we were interrupted by the reappearance of the vicar, supported by his wife. His face was ashen, but he seemed less troubled. "I am sorry," he said. "I never intended to sleep for so long."

"Please don't apologise," said my friend. "Now that you are up and about, you really must try and eat something. Don't you agree, Doctor?"

"Yes, most certainly you should," said I.

"Come along to the kitchen, dearest," said the vicar's wife. "I will prepare you something."

When they had gone, the Inspector also took his leave, promising to be back first thing in the morning. Holmes and I sat in the study, for some time, in silence.

When the vicar returned, with his wife, there was some colour in his cheeks which had been wholly absent before. Clearly he had managed to eat something.

"It is my unpleasant duty," said Holmes, "in the absence of the Inspector, to tell you that the sexton, also, has been murdered."

The clergyman wept openly, and was comforted by his wife.

Holmes and I rose to leave, but the vicar motioned us to remain. "Please, Mr. Holmes, and you, Doctor Watson, will you stay here, at least for tonight."

"We would be delighted to stay," said my friend. "In any case, it was a favour that I was going to ask of you."

We passed a quiet, and rather solemn evening. The vicar did not seem inclined to discuss the sad events, and Holmes and I did not encourage him to do so. About ten, Holmes and I went to our room, where there were two beds separated by a small table. Holmes placed upon the table, next to the candlestick, the key we had found in the murdered sexton's hand, a lantern and a box of vestas. Then he blew out the candle, and I heard the creak of the bedsprings as he lay down to rest.

I been asleep for some time when a sound awakened me, and I was surprised to find my friend dressing by candlelight.

"Whatever are you doing, Holmes?" I whispered.

"I must go out," he replied. "There is nothing you can do to help me. On this occasion I must go alone."

With that he departed, taking the objects which he had placed upon the table with him. I looked at my watch and saw that it was ten minutes after midnight. I blew out the candle, and after a time, drifted back to sleep. When next I awoke, it was daylight, and my friend was not in the room. The lantern was on the table once more, showing that he had been back, and gone out again.

At breakfast there was still no sign of Holmes, but he came into the dining room as we were coming to the end of the meal. He refused all offers of food, but consumed a whole pot of coffee. He radiated that nervous energy that I had seen many times before: it meant that he could see light at the end of the tunnel. I knew then, that his expedition of the night before had borne fruit.

"What are your plans now, Mr. Holmes?" enquired the vicar, after Holmes had settled back in his chair and lit his pipe.

"Doctor Watson and I must, unfortunately, leave for London by the next available train," replied my friend. "It has not proved to be an easy case," continued Holmes, "and I have a multitude of things to see to in London. I shall certainly be in touch again, within the next few weeks."

"Very well then," said the clergyman. "I thank you for the time which you have already spent looking into these matters."

"I have explained the position to the Inspector this morning," said Holmes. "I believe he understands."

It was not long before Holmes and I were in a train rattling back to London. I broke the silence which had fallen upon us in the carriage. "Do you not think, Holmes, that you were somewhat abrupt in your treatment of the vicar before we left?"

"I am sorry for that," replied Holmes, "but I had a very good reason for making him think we were no further forward in our investigation. I have given the Inspector the same impression."

"Can you tell me the reason?" I asked.

"Quite simply - I do not wish to alert the murderer in any way."

"Did the Inspector's men find out anything last night?"

"No," said Holmes, "they did not, but then again I did not think they would. And before you ask, Watson, I have to tell you that my own nocturnal expedition did not have anything in common with theirs. I am afraid that I cannot tell you anything about it at this juncture. However, all will become clear in a little over six days time."

On our arrival in London, Holmes hailed a cab, and we drove back to Baker Street. We stopped once on the way, at

Stanford's, the map people. Holmes emerged bearing a cardboard tube, containing, I presumed, a large scale map of the area from which we had just come.

When we arrived at our lodgings, I expected Holmes to unfurl the map and pore over it for hours. He surprised me by tossing it on to the top of a cupboard and then engaging me in conversation for some little time on the manufacture of violins in general, and those of Amati in particular. That evening, I attempted once again to draw him out about the case in hand, but he answered my questions with mono-syllables, and was particularly reticent when I asked him why there would be a delay of six days before anything more could be done.

The days passed, and I felt an increasing sense of tension. My companion, however, seemed to become more and more calm. On the penultimate day, just after breakfast, Holmes took down the cardboard tube and unrolled the map on the table. It proved to be, indeed, a large scale map of the area, with the village more or less in the centre. Holmes spent a great deal of time examining the map, murmuring to himself and making notes, which I was not allowed to see. He then sent off a couple of telegrams, received one in return, and announced to me that his plans were finalised.

That morning Holmes had received a letter containing details of the Leavis murder, of infamous repute (which, by the way, he was eventually entirely successful in clearing up, thus preventing the wrongful indictment of the nobleman concerned).

Late in the afternoon of the final day, Holmes and I once again entrained for Sussex, and when we reached the village halt of Fletcham, I was surprised that this was our destination, as it was two stops up the line from Lampton. We were met by Inspector Pringle, who greeted us warmly.

We repaired to the inn, where the Inspector had taken a room for each of us. This was to be our centre for the coming night. After we had dined, we went up to the Inspector's room, and Holmes outlined his plans. He again unfurled the map which he had brought with him and began by showing that, owing to the fact that the railway curved to follow a valley, we were only about a mile from Lampton as the crow flies, to the west of that parish.

As we sat, smoking our pipes, Holmes explained that at about eleven we were to leave the inn, and make our way to a wood on the squire's land, about a quarter of a mile north of his house. The Inspector had arranged that six of his most reliable men, were to conceal themselves in the wood at strategic points at the time we were to leave the inn.

Time crept by after Holmes finished speaking, conversation languished into silence, only broken by the creak of chairs, coals settling in the grate, and the knocking out of pipes.

At last the hour arrived, and we all put on our coats and made our way, as quietly as we could, downstairs. We managed to get past the tap room without arousing anyone's attention, and soon found ourselves on the road outside. This road took us some of the way, but soon we left it and started up a rough track, at the end of which were some ruined farm buildings, beyond them lay open countryside. Holmes took a bearing by the light of a match, using a pocket compass which he had brought, and we followed this bearing across some fields. Now and then we could hear the crunching sound of animals grazing, together with their heavy breath, and the swish of their tails.

It was a cloudy night with a keen wind and some drizzle, we were helped a little on our trek by the brief appearances, between the clouds, of the moon in its second quarter.

At length we came to the wood shown on the map, Holmes led the way to the centre of it, through the dripping trees. At one point our nerves were stretched to an almost unbearable tautness, by the sudden appearance of a man from the bushes at

23

the side of the path, he proved, however, to be one of the Inspector's men, and after a brief discussion in whispers, he concealed himself once more, and we continued on our way.

In the centre of the wood, we could just make out a large, dark mass. On closer inspection it turned out to be a stone-built barn, or storehouse, the great double door of the place was open, and we cautiously made our way inside. Using the light of a lantern, which the Inspector had brought, we took stock of our surroundings. The building housed a considerable collection of junk, both household and agricultural, there were broken down old carts, discarded pieces of furniture, ploughs, harnesses and the like, besides a quantity of hay or straw. It became clear that we were waiting for the arrival of someone, when Holmes suggested that we conceal ourselves behind a battered, old, two-wheeled cart, which rested on its shafts in one corner of the building. Once we reached this place, we made ourselves as comfortable as we could. It was now a little before midnight.

The Inspector told us, in a whisper, that his men had orders to allow any person or persons to enter the wood, but they were to arrest and hold anyone leaving. The man who had come out at us in the wood would be severely reproved for disobeying that instruction.

We waited in our place of concealment in total darkness, and then Holmes, sitting between us, stiffened and gave each a warning shake. I was conscious of a draught, and at the same time heard the sound of the door opening, and then closing. Someone had come into the barn. This same someone then struck a match, and lit a candle which stood in its holder on a table in the middle of the building. It was a woman, wearing a hooded, black cloak. She remained only long enough at the table to light the candle, and disappeared somewhere into the shadows. Some time passed, and then the door was slowly and cautiously opened again, this time there was enough light from the candle to make out the entry of a tall, thick-set man. The woman sprang from the shadows as soon as he closed the door behind him, and flung herself into his arms.

"Oh, Tom," she cried, "I've been so worried about you. Not being able to see you for a week has been such hell."

"I would never have stayed away from you so long, had you not wished it, Sarah," he replied.

"Tom!" she cried, distressed. "You know I had to tell you to stay away! It was for your own safety, the police were everywhere. As it was, you took a fearful risk in meeting me here at our usual time last week."

"I should never have killed him," said Tom bitterly. "I only did it because I could not bear to spend so little time with you."

"I never asked you to kill him!" she exclaimed. "I thought that we were going to run away together. I never dreamed that the church bell was part of your plan. I thought it was someone's idea of a joke, and I feel so sorry for the poor sexton, he had never harmed anybody."

"I too am sorry for that," replied Tom, "but as long as I live, I will never be sorry for that brute of a husband of yours. If we had run away, he would have come after us wherever we went."

At this point Holmes nudged us both sharply in the ribs: a prearranged signal. The Inspector rose silently to his feet, and took a few steps forward before speaking.

"Mr. Thomas Edginton, I arrest you for the murders of ..."

He got no further. At the first sound of his voice, the couple whirled round with shock, a look of terror came over the face of the man and he ran out of the barn. The woman, with a loud exhalation of breath, collapsed into a heap. We approached the unconscious woman, and I arranged her into a more comfortable position.

"My men will get him, Mr. Holmes," said the Inspector grimly. "Have no fear about that."

Hardly were these words out of his mouth, when we heard a lot of shouting in the distance, and soon Thomas Edginton made his second appearance in the barn that night, this time surrounded by six men in plain clothes, and with his hands handcuffed behind his back.

"As I was saying," said the Inspector imperturbably. "Mr. Thomas Edginton, I arrest you for the murders of Squire Benfield and Mr. Joshua Edwards, the sexton."

On hearing this, the arrested man made a brief and futile attempt to struggle free. He was a strong man, and it was some little time before he was finally subdued.

"Good work, men," said the Inspector after he became quiet. "Take him away."

After they had gone, we turned our attention to the woman, who was showing signs of regaining consciousness. As soon as she did so, she burst into hysterical weeping. We half-carried her back to the squire's house, and a servant was dispatched to fetch her doctor, as I did not have my medical bag with me.

The Inspector had arranged for an unmarked carriage to wait outside the inn and we were soon taken back to the inn at Fletcham. It was a short journey, during which nobody spoke.

When we arrived, we all trooped upstairs, and gathered, once again, in the Inspector's room.

"A very pretty piece of work, Mr. Holmes," said the Inspector after we had settled ourselves, "but I must confess that I am still very much in the dark as to how you managed it."

"I would not have been able to manage it, as you put it," said my friend, "were it not for the use of imagination and a stroke of good fortune. You will remember, Watson, that I used the same technique in the case of Silver Blaze: I imagined what might have happened to the horse, and then acted upon it. You will probably also recall, Watson, that when we stayed with the vicar that night, I got up and went out at about midnight?"

"Yes," I replied. "I remember it well."

"The Inspector had told us earlier that evening, about the squire's brutality to his wife. I was moved then to try a long shot, two long shots in fact. The first was the idea that the squire's wife might have taken a lover, because of her husband's cavalier treatment of her. It occurred to me that if that was the case, they had to meet somewhere, and that some-where could not, obviously, be the residence of the lady, or of the gentleman. Further, the meeting place was more likely to be nearer the lady's house than the gentleman's. The reason for this assumption was that she could not risk being out of the marital home for long, whereas the gentleman would be a free agent, and his time would be his own. This assumption was based on the idea that the gentleman was himself unmarried, but I thought it was unlikely that he had a wife."

"And what was the second long shot?" I asked.

"The second long shot was that the key which we found, might, just might, be that for the meeting place itself, and, if my first assumption was true, it could very well be on land belonging to the squire. I therefore decided to carry out a reconnaissance in the environs of the squire's house."

"At midnight, Holmes," I exclaimed.

"Yes, I wanted to see if the key which we found would fit any of the locks of outbuildings on the squire's land, which I could hardly do by daylight, without attracting attention. Anyway, I gave the murder scene a wide berth, for I knew that the Inspector's men were keeping watch there, and I approached the house from opposite that place. I had tried the key in the locks of two of the furthest flung outbuildings, when I woke the dog, which, fortunately for me, was chained. I should add that the house itself was in darkness. I retreated into the shadows.

"Soon after the dog began to bark, a door of the house opened and the figure of a man carrying a lantern appeared, I was at a distance of perhaps fifty yards from this door. Luckily for me, the man did not seem to think there was any cause for alarm, and, after spending a few moments with the animal, to calm it, he went back indoors.

"I retraced my steps to a point where I had a good view of the squire's house and adjoining land, and in the distance, somewhat to the north, I heard a sound, as of the slamming of a door, it came from the middle of the very woods where we were tonight. This is where the stroke of good fortune came into play. I carefully made my way towards the source of the sound, and discovered the barn where the melodrama which we witnessed tonight was enacted.

"I crept up to the double doors of the barn, and heard two people, a man and a woman, in agitated conversation. I heard enough of this conversation to ascertain that the man was the murderer, and that the woman was the squire's wife. I heard them make arrangements to meet a week from that night, at one in the morning.

"When it became obvious that they were ready to depart, I left the barn, and took up a position some distance from it. The woman went back the way she came, carrying a lantern. The man, also with a lantern, went due north, and I made mental note to examine a large scale map of the area, to see what lay in that direction. It transpired, when I did so, that there was only one group of buildings in that direction, within a mile or so: those of Edginton's farm. I advised the Inspector of this by wire, and he was able to deploy his men in such a way that they were some distance from the route that Edginton must take to reach the barn, so that the chances of their being discovered by him, and so giving the game away, were slight.

"Also, after they had gone, I tried the key in the lock of the barn door. It fitted. Of course, after the loss of the key, they were obliged to abandon the idea of keeping the place locked, and instead, left it open. They were certainly safe from discovery by the squire, after his murder, in any case. Even had they removed the lock from the door, and disposed of it, it would not, as it happens, have changed the course of events tonight in any way."

"There, Mr. Holmes," said the Inspector. "A pretty piece of work, as I have said, and I shall go further than that. It was masterly, and I owe you yet another apology for ever having doubted you and your methods."

"Yes, Holmes," I added. "It was a brilliant piece of detective work, and I congratulate you."

Holmes showed evident signs of pleasure at these accolades. "Gentlemen," said Holmes. "I thank you for your appreciation, but I fear that it is very late, and the best thing now would be if we all retired for the night. If there are any other points you want clarified, Inspector, I would be glad to go over them with you tomorrow morning."

"Watson, I shall be glad of your assistance when we get back to Baker Street tomorrow in the matter of the Leavis case."

The Adventure of Polly Winthrop

I had persuaded my friend, Mr. Sherlock Holmes, to take a few days' holiday in a Sussex seaside town. This proved a very difficult task, but partly because things were very quiet in London, and partly because we had been assisting at the coroner's court in Tunbridge Wells, and had been half-way there, so to speak, I had prevailed.

We found a charming little hotel in a secluded spot towards one end of the town, where we could be assured of some peace and quiet. For the first twenty-four hours, Holmes displayed a complete indifference to my solicitations for his welfare, he had been working very hard, up until a few weeks ago, on the case which had culminated in the coroner's court, but could not see why I thought that he should take a complete break, and said so.

He had told Mrs. Hudson, in no uncertain terms, that if anything should come up while he was away, she must telegraph him at once.

Now however, on the second day, his impatience with everything his new surroundings had to offer was wearing off, and the heartache, which he always evidenced when he was away from Baker Street for any length of time, was showing signs of lessening.

For myself, I felt like one who holds one's breath, in the anticipation of something pleasant or unpleasant, as in this case. I hoped with all my strength, that the days we spent here would not be cut short by a wire from London. This feeling was based entirely upon my concern for my friend, which, so far, had been wasted on him.

We had just dined, that second evening, and we were enjoying a glass of brandy in the bar, when, at the far side of the room, an argument broke out between two men. A young woman, who was obviously the sweetheart of the younger of the two men, implored him to come away, which, after the exchange of a few more angry words with the older man, he did, and they left the hotel together.

"I wonder what that was about," said Holmes, his interest aroused. He had, by this time, mellowed somewhat in his attitude towards his exile from London, and with that mellowing, had come his old enemy: boredom.

He turned to a red-faced man of genial appearance, who was sitting at the table next to us, and, having begged his pardon for speaking to him without being introduced, asked him if he knew anything about the contretemps we had just witnessed.

"Bless you, sir," said the red-faced man, "indeed I do know all about it, for it is common knowledge in these parts. You must be strangers, both of you, not to know."

"What then?" asked Holmes.

"'Tis a long story, sir. Can I sit at your table for the telling of it?"

Holmes nodded his acquiescence, disregarding a sharp tug which I gave, covertly, at the sleeve of his jacket.

The red-faced man sat at our table, bringing his stone mug of ale with him.

"This is my friend and colleague, Doctor Watson," said Holmes, waving his hand in my direction. "My name is Sherlock Holmes."

It was clear from the red-faced man's unchanged demeanour, that he had never heard of either of us. It was also clear that Holmes was enjoying my discomfiture at this turn of events.

"How d'you do," said I, shaking his hand with a heartiness I did not feel, and casting an inimical glance at Holmes.

"George Tippet," said the red-faced man, "very pleased to meet you, I'm sure." He shook Holmes' hand. Then, taking a long pull at his mug, and wiping his mouth with the back of his hand, he began.

"Well, sirs, until about a year ago, there was to the north of this town, a cab company which ran a service to and from the railway station, supplied carriages for weddings and funerals, and suchlike. I say was, because they are no longer in business and for reasons you shall hear shortly.

"The cab company was run by Josiah Winthrop, and his daughter, Polly. Josiah made no secret of the fact that he disliked his daughter and his little mouse of a wife. The wife, for not giving him a son to carry on the business, the daughter, simply because she was a girl. Yet Polly did all she could to please him, and proved to have a flair for business, besides driving the cabs and carriages, when the need arose. They had two other drivers as well.

"Polly met a young man from this town, by way of business, you might say, but their relationship soon turned to one of a romantic nature. Josiah was dead set against him from the start: he thought him a worthless, idling, ne'er-do-well, and he forbade Polly from having anything to do with him, on pain of his severe displeasure. But Polly loved him, and continued to see him secretly, she would tell as how she did not have much fun in life anyway, and that her father's irritation was something she had to live with, whether she tried to please him or no.

"Polly's young man was in here to-day, sirs, he being the one that the younger man and lady was arguing with, and you shall presently know from me the reason why.

"You should know also, that Polly had another admirer, a man she had known since childhood, everybody always thought that he and Polly were made for each other, and that one day they would be wed. He was a farmer's son, name of Broadbent - Jim Broadbent. The farm was a prosperous one, and he stood to inherit it when his father died, for he was an only child. Polly's father thought the world of him, and besides, was an old friend of Jim's father."

32

Here he paused to take a sip of ale and I stole a glance at Holmes. He was listening with rapt attention, and patience - not normally one of his greatest virtues. He was, I supposed, like a man, who when starving, will eat the most meagre and unappetising fare, and be grateful for it.

Our red-faced acquaintance continued with his narrative. "And so, sirs, all seemed set fair for Polly and Jim, until this other man came into her life. Everything was now changed. Whereas she and Jim had been almost inseparable, now they quarrelled, and she made it clear to him that she could barely stand him. I tell you, it fair broke his heart, and he could not understand why Polly was so against him all of a sudden.

"The thing is, Polly kept the fact that she had a new beau a secret from everyone, including Jim, and she was especially careful not to give her father a clue as to what was going on. The name of her new man was Dick Knight, but there was nothing of shining armour about that one.

"And now, we come to that terrible night, which led to the downfall of poor Jim Broadbent, and the end of the cab company. Just after midnight, on a rainy and windy night, there came a knocking at the door of an inn to the north, outside the town, an inn called the Blue Posts. Well the place had shut up for the night, and the landlord leaned out of the window, to tell whoever was there to go away, and let him have his sleep, when, to his surprise he heard a woman crying, and obviously in a bad state. It was Polly, whom he knew well.

"Anyway, he hurried downstairs to let her in, and when she came into the light, he saw, to his horror, that she was bleeding from scratches on her face and neck, and her clothes were torn, covered with mud, and bedraggled, she being soaked to the skin. She just managed to tell him that she had been attacked on her way home after her last fare, before she collapsed on the floor in a dead faint.

"Well, the doctor was called to her and they made her comfortable for the night. The next morning she had recovered enough to tell her story.

"It seems that she had been driving a light chaise that night, had dropped off her last fare on the outskirts of town, and was on her way home, when, on a lonely stretch of road, a man, muffled up against the weather, stepped out of some bushes, and held up the cab. She was stricken with fear at his appearance, she said, since she had the week's takings with her in a leather bag, which she had not yet paid into the bank.

"Her worst fears were realised when the stranger pulled her roughly from the driving seat, threw her to the ground, and, using violence, forced her to disclose the whereabouts of the money. He took this, then loosed the horse from the harnesses, pushed the chaise on its side, and set fire to it, afterwards making off into the night, in the direction of town. Polly managed to stagger across some fields, a short cut, to the Blue Posts, a distance of about half a mile.

"Of course, sirs, a big hue and cry was set up by this, the chaise was found in the place which she had spoken of, partly destroyed by fire, and there were ample signs of a struggle. Pieces of torn clothing were found, which were matched to the clothes she had worn that night.

"And now, sirs, I come to a most distressing part of this sorry business. Jim had been in the Blue Posts that night, and had left, the worse for drink, about an hour before Polly got there. He had found out about Polly and Dick that very day, had said terrible things about Polly, and moreover, had vowed to have his revenge on one or the other of them before much more time passed. Nobody paid much attention to this at the time, except that they were shocked to see him drink so much - he was normally the most sober of men - and hear him speak in such a way. They assumed that it was the drink talking, as

34

you might say, that he was grieved by the news about Polly and Dick, and not quite in his right mind.

"Anyway, Jim got back at the farm very late that night, at some time in the small hours, and one of the servants noticed, that, when he let him in, he was in a dirty and dishevelled state, his hands had cuts on them, and he was wet through.

"Word gets around quickly in these parts and it was only the following afternoon when the police came to arrest him. He protested his innocence, then and to the last, but he was convicted at the assizes, and given ten years. The judge told him that his sentence would have been much more severe, but for his previous good character.

"When Polly heard of his arrest, she had a fit of screaming, and went into a complete collapse, she was confined to her bed, and she is there still. She and her father are reconciled now, and he looks after her as if she were a baby. The cab company is no more, and her father's own health is ruined. He has become a white-haired shambling wreck of the fine figure that once he was. He blames himself for the terrible events of that night, swearing that they would never have happened had he been kinder to his daughter, and discouraged her from playing a part in the business."

"Tell me," said Holmes, who was now alert and intent, in the way I knew so well, "was the money ever recovered?"

"Bless you sir, no, it was never found."

"Did the police interview Dick Knight?"

"They went to his house, but he swore he had come home that evening at eight o'clock, just about the time it started to rain. He lived with his aunt and uncle, his parents being dead, and they backed up his story. Some money was found in his room, but it weren't the cab takings.

"How did they ascertain that?" asked Holmes.

"Well, sir, it was in currency notes, just under ten pound,

with only a few shillings in coin. The takings was all in silver and coppers."

"And I suppose nothing of the kind was found at Broadbent's house?"

"No, sir, as I said, the money was never found."

"Did not the fact that this money was not found at Broadbent's house, go any way towards clearing his name at the trial?" asked Holmes.

"No, sir, it did not, they made out that he could have hidden it, before he went home that night."

"What account did Broadbent give for his movements after he left the Blue Posts?"

"Well, sir, he said that after he left, he went on to the heath for a walk to clear his head before going home. His father never did hold with drink. He said he fell down a couple of times, on account of the roughness of the ground, cutting his hands on stones, and scratching them on the gorse bushes."

Holmes was silent for a time after this. Then he said, quietly and slowly, almost to himself, "Jim Broadbent is a very unlucky man."

"Yes, sir," said the red-faced man, "unlucky in love, and then this."

"And I suppose," said Holmes, almost as an afterthought, "that Polly did not notice anything about her assailant which would have enabled her to identify him?"

"No, sir, she swore that she didn't know him from Adam."

"By the way," said Holmes, "who were the young couple, those two who were quarrelling with Dick Knight?"

"That was Jim's cousin and her young man. They believe Jim is innocent, and that Dick knows more about that night than he is telling."

A silence fell at this point, and the red-faced rose to take his leave of us, and, almost as an afterthought, Holmes flipped a half-sovereign on to the table in front of him. The man's eyes widened with surprise, and a pleased expression suffused his ruddy features.

"Thanking you kindly, sir," he said, touching his cap.

"I would be glad if you could show me on the morrow where the attack took place," said Holmes.

"With pleasure, sir. I'll be in here about ten in the morning, if that meets with your approval, sir." He had become much more amenable on being presented with the gold coin.

Holmes nodded. "Ten it is then."

Later we sat up in Holmes's room, smoking our pipes. I felt a lingering resentment at Holmes's readiness to listen to such a story as we had listened to that evening, when he was supposed to be recuperating.

I unfairly blamed the red-faced man, and as a result, did not look forward to the next day's expedition, but the real culprit was Holmes himself, whose interest had been aroused by the quarrel in the bar, and who had sensed that it concerned something of note.

"I sometimes despair of you, Holmes." I said, somewhat more sharply than I intended.

Holmes looked at me in surprise. "Why, Watson, whatever is the matter?"

"Perhaps you have forgotten. We are supposed to be here for the benefit of your health, and now you are preparing to investigate a case which was closed months ago."

"Hardly an investigation," said Holmes, with a slight smile. "And besides, what is wrong with a little conversation of an evening, and a brisk walk in the sea air after breakfast tomorrow?"

I gave it up, I should have remembered that there was no point in remonstrating with Holmes at the best of times, and never less so than now, when his mind was obviously made up.

"I suppose then, that I shall have to put up with you taxing your mind with this affair, a case which is obviously cut and dried, when complete rest would be the thing."

"On the contrary," said he, "I shall not be taxing my mind, as you put it, because I have already solved this case, and the truth of it is very different from that which has been accepted."

I was relieved, in the first place, to hear this, and then surprised that Holmes thought there was more to the matter than met the eye, but I knew better than to press him for details.

The next morning, after breakfast, we once again found ourselves in the company of Tippet, and after exchanging a few pleasantries, we set off to view the scene of the attack. It was a sunny day, with a slight breeze, and I comforted myself with the notion that we were at least taking some exercise in the open air, and that this could not fail to do my friend some good.

Little was said by any of us, and when we reached the spot, Holmes gave Tippet another half-sovereign, and bade him good morning, much to my relief.

"You know where to find me if you want me," said Tippet, over his shoulder, as he went back towards town, whistling, and swinging his stick.

There were but a few traces left of the attack, which had taken place at the junction of three roads, a slight bareness, where the grass had been scorched, and partially grown again, some pieces of charcoal, and a few rusty nails and screws. I really could not see what Holmes hoped to gain by this visit, but I resolved not to ask. Tippet had told us, before he left, that besides the road which led back to town, one led past the Broadbent farmstead, about half a mile distant, while the other led past the residence of the Winthrops, also about half a mile away, so that the two places were about a mile apart.

Holmes spent quite a bit of time sifting through the remains of the fire, afterwards he started to beat around in nearby bushes with his stick. He then dug up some earth, from a spot about twenty yards from the fire, and, having wrapped it in waxed paper, he placed it in his pocket. Finally he systematically prodded the ground, deeply, with his stick, at intervals of about a foot, until he had covered the ground for a radius of about twenty feet around the site of the fire. Finally, he straightened up, appearing a little disappointed. He had obviously not found whatever it was that he was seeking.

"What now, Holmes?" I asked, rather puzzled by his actions, especially those concerning the earth.

"I think we will go and have a glass of ale at the Blue Posts," said he.

The inn was quite a large establishment, set beside a stream in a little wooded valley. It was fairly hidden from view, and we had had some difficulty finding it, but eventually we found ourselves in the almost deserted bar, sparsely furnished with a few tables and chairs, set upon bare boards. We each decided to try a glass of the local ale.

"That was a bad business you had here about a year ago," said Holmes to the landlord, who had emerged from behind the bar, to clear an adjacent table of empty pots.

The landlord looked narrowly at Holmes, and seemed about to say something hostile, but then he checked himself, perhaps it was my companion's open and friendly expression, or perhaps it was because we were both so obviously gentlemen.

"You mean that business with Polly Winthrop, I suppose," he said, in a guarded tone.

"Just so," said Holmes.

"Well, I got my own views about that," said the landlord.

"Really," said my friend, "and what would they be?"

Again the landlord considered my friend carefully, and when he spoke he was almost conspiratorial. "Well, sir, I never thought that Jim Broadbent had anything to do with it, he were a good lad, I've known him since he were a boy, and it was a crying shame what happened to him. It's my opinion that Dick Knight knows more'n he's telling, and a lot of folk around here feel the same."

Holmes received this impassively.

"Polly swore it weren't him, at the trial, but it didn't do no good, she was in a bad state, she had to give her evidence from a bed, and everybody thought she seemed confused, and not in her right mind."

Holmes nodded.

"Can I ask you sir, what's your interest in this - I mean, are you acting for anybody?"

"Let us just say that I'm on Jim Broadbent's side," said Holmes.

The shadow, which had hung over the landlord's countenance since the beginning of the conversation, lifted at this, and he shook Holmes's hand.

"Then good luck to you, sir," said the landlord, "and if there is anything I can do..."

"There is one thing," said my friend.

"Just name it," said the landlord.

"Do you know where can I borrow a dog with a good nose, just for an afternoon?"

The landlord was taken aback by this, and, for a moment, he seemed to think that my companion was having a joke at his expense. "Are you serious?" he said.

"I assure you, I have never been more so," said Holmes.

"Well then, what you need is old Billy Brockley's dog - Jinty, he calls it. He uses it for mole-catching."

"When may I borrow it?" asked my friend.

"Well, he always calls in of an evening, I'll tell him that you want to borrow it, and he'll probably let you have it tomorrow afternoon."

"Right you are," said Holmes, "I shall be in tomorrow at twelve, and I'll take the dog then. I shall probably need it for only an hour or two, in any case."

So saying, he drained his glass, motioned me to do the same, and bade the landlord good day. As we left, the few people there eyed us with great curiosity.

Holmes and I strolled back to town, he was deep in thought, and I too had my own thoughts to contend with. What was it, for instance, that Holmes could see in all this, which remained dark to me? And why on earth did he want a tracking dog? Surely any scent, or scents, that might have helped him, had long ago disappeared.

The brightness of the June day intruded upon these and other thoughts, and I gave myself over to the complete enjoyment of everything it offered to my senses.

At the outskirts of town we parted, Holmes headed for the town centre, and I went back to the hotel.

I had just finished dressing for dinner, when there was a tap at the door. When I opened it, Holmes entered, he was carrying two or three small packets done up in brown paper and string.

"I just thought I would tell you that I am back," said he. "I shall be ready to go down to dinner in twenty minutes."

Dinner that evening was a sombre affair, Holmes spoke very little, and took so long over the soup, that it became cold and congealed, and had to be removed. He was as preoccupied as I had ever seen him. I tried to speak to him, but he answered in monosyllables, sometimes a few minutes after I had spoken. The conversation languished, if indeed it could have been said to be alive in the first place.

We were on the point of leaving the table, when a strapping thick-set man came into the restaurant, and made his way over to us. I recognised him as the man we had seen on the previous evening, arguing with the young couple. He was Dick Knight.

"What do you mean by going around asking questions about Polly," he stormed, without preamble, shaking his fist.

The other diners turned to stare at this commotion.

Holmes leaned back in his chair, with a sardonic smile. "Why, Mr. Knight," he said, "anyone would think that you had something to hide."

This took some of the wind from his sails. "I had nothing to do with what happened that night," he said in a quieter tone.

Holmes nodded. "I know that you did not, at least not directly."

This seemed to perplex him, and he became calmer still, or perhaps more confused.

"Well, just keep your nose out of what doesn't concern you."

"It is a free country, is it not?" said my friend.

Knight seemed to be, suddenly, in the grip of some strong emotion, but then he turned on his heel, and left without another word. He must have realised that Holmes was not to be intimidated

"An unpleasant young man," said Holmes, imperturbably.

I glanced around the restaurant, the stares were beginning to die down, but I still felt uncomfortable.

We had a drink in the bar, before retiring, and I was glad to note that the red-faced man was nowhere to be seen.

The following afternoon saw us back at the place of the fire, but this time we had the dog, Jinty, with us. Jinty was one of those medium-sized dogs of indeterminate breed, brindled and good-natured. He had gone with us very readily, mouth open and tongue lolling, after we left the Blue Posts, wearing a new collar which Holmes had purchased the previous afternoon, together with a new leash.

As soon as we reached that place, Holmes had taken something out of waxed paper, and given it to him to scent, afterwards re-wrapping it in the paper and placing a large stone over

42

it. He had his back to me when he did this, so I did not see what he had used. Then we set off through a hedge into a neighbouring field along a line which led to the Blue Posts.

When we got to within ten yards of a copse which lay in our path, the dog showed signs of excitement and began to strain at the leash. Once we were in the copse, about two hundred yards from our starting point, he started to dig, quivering with excitement. In no time at all he had unearthed something which had been buried a few inches beneath the surface, some kind of material, partly decomposed by its interment. It proved to be a leather bag, filled with discoloured silver and copper coins.

"Holmes!" I exclaimed, "this is remarkable! How did you know of its existence?"

"I anticipated it, I expected to find it. It had to be hidden somewhere between the scene of the fire and the Blue Posts."

"Then the story Polly told was not true."

"I never thought that it was."

"Do you now know the identity of Polly's assailant?"

"Polly was not attacked by anyone that night."

"What! But the torn clothes, the fire, her distress."

"She did it all herself"

"But why?"

"That I do not know for the moment, but I shall find out."

Holmes patted the dog, which was now sitting, panting after his exertions, beside the hole which he had dug. Having taken possession of the bag of money, Holmes and I walked back to the scene of the fire, and the dog walked happily with us. Holmes lifted the stone, picked up the package and removed the waxed paper, to reveal a wet leather bag, containing a few shillings and coppers, together with a little earth.

"I bought this bag yesterday," he said, "and having placed some loose change, and the earth I collected from this spot in it,

I left it soaking in a bowl of water overnight, so that a reaction could take place between the leather, the earth and the coins, in the hope that it would produce a scent similar to the one I was seeking. It would seem that my expectations were justified."

"Yes, of course," said I, still slightly shaken by the turn of events.

We returned to the Blue Posts, and Holmes presented the dog, complete with collar and lead, to old Billy Brockley.

We were, once again, the cynosure of all the eyes in the place, especially when Holmes gave old Billy a half-sovereign for his trouble. The old man's nut-brown features cracked into a grin at this, a grin which revealed only two or three teeth.

"Any time you gents wants ter borrow Jinty," he said, "you only has ter ask." He then leaned down, and allowed Jinty to finish off the ale in his mug.

Holmes nodded to the landlord, who returned it in silence, and then we took our leave. Holmes strode so quickly from the Blue Posts, that I assumed he had a definite purpose in mind. For the moment, however, I decided not to ask what it might be, and I simply tagged along.

The day was fine and bright, and presently a excellent view of the sea presented itself through the trees, together with a few sailing ships. I tried to draw Holmes's attention to this, but he just shrugged, and carried on with the same determination.

We soon found ourselves back at the junction of three roads where the carriage fire had taken place. At this point Holmes took the road which led to the former Winthrop cab company. It was evident that he was going to take the bull by the horns and confront Polly with the money bag which we had found by such curious means.

At length we came upon a large, detached house, set back from the road, with a cobbled courtyard to the front. Fringing this courtyard were a number of outbuildings, some of which were obviously stables. Near the apex of one of the roofs of the buildings was a sign which had been painted out with white-wash. This had weathered, and it was just possible to read the legend: WINTHROP CABS AND CARRIAGES.

The entrance to the courtyard was via a five-barred gate, and this Holmes now opened, allowing us to make our way to the house itself. As we approached the front door, the sound of many dogs barking fell upon our ears. Fortunately for us, these dogs must have been securely tethered, or otherwise confined, because they did not present themselves to our sight. But the feeling that they might appear at any moment persisted and it was not a pleasant prospect.

Holmes rapped loudly at the door, and also pulled at the bell. There was no response to either of these actions for some minutes, and I began to think that we had had a wasted journey.

We were just about to leave, when a window above our heads opened, and the head and shoulders of an elderly, grey-haired man emerged. "What do you want?" he said, in a surprisingly loud voice, considering the frailty which his first appearance suggested.

"My name is Sherlock Holmes," said my companion, "and this is my friend, Doctor Watson. We have come to see Polly, on a matter of the utmost importance."

"I have never heard of either of you, and my Polly is too unwell to see anybody," retorted the elderly man.

"I have heard it said that you are an honourable man," replied Holmes. "I appeal to your honour now, so that a man who has been wrongfully imprisoned, a man for whom you held, and perhaps still hold, the greatest esteem, can be freed."

"I do not know of whom you speak," said the elderly man.

"Does the name Jim Broadbent mean anything to you?"

"What does he have to do with your presence here?" said the elderly man, with some scorn.

"Everything!" shouted Holmes. "The story your daughter told you of the night she was attacked is not true and I can prove it. I thought it best that the truth should come from her own lips before we go to the police."

"The police!" said the elderly man, then, after a pause, "How can you prove what Polly told of that night is wrong?"

For answer, Holmes held up the tattered leather bag of money, which he had kept concealed under his coat, and said: "We have found the money which Polly said was stolen, and it was hidden in a place which is totally at odds with her account."

The elderly man was silent for almost a minute after this, and then he seemed to come to a resolution. "Be off with you!" he shouted, "or by God I will set the dogs on you!"

"Very well then," said my friend composedly, "we shall go, but I warn you, this is not the end of the matter."

As we made our way back down the courtyard, the barking, which had been incessant throughout our conversation with the elderly man, suddenly became more frantic.

Scarcely had we closed and latched the gate, than they appeared, running towards us. We quickened our steps, and made our way back to town, and I executed many a backward glance to ensure that they were not following us.

"Well, really!" said I, when I realised we were safe, "what a way to behave."

"I rather thought that it might be difficult to see Polly," said Holmes, distantly. Still, we have other avenues open to us."

"We must go to the police the moment we arrive back in town," I declared.

"No," said my friend, "we shall put that off until the morrow. For now we shall content ourselves with the knowledge that we did try to do the right thing."

The following morning after breakfast found us in Holmes's room. We were preparing to go to the police with the bag of money, and an account of how we found it, when there was a knock at the door.

When I opened it, I saw a young woman in a faded black dress and hat, leaning heavily on a stick. She seemed, to my practised eye, to be suffering from some kind of wasting disease.

She was etiolated, severely thin and underweight, and had great shadows under her eyes. "My name is Polly Winthrop," she announced in the whispery voice of someone whose vitality is reduced to a critical level.

I ushered her in, and we gave her a seat at the window.

"My father is downstairs," she continued. "He was very much opposed to my coming here, and it was only with the greatest difficulty that I persuaded him to bring me, and to speak to you alone. I must tell you that I overheard the whole of your conversation with my father yesterday, and when I heard that you had found the money, God alone knows how, which I thought I had hidden so carefully, my blood turned to water. I got out of my bed and carefully peeped through the curtains, and when I saw the bag, I realised that I could keep my shameful secret no longer."

"How did you know where to find us?" asked Holmes.

"It wasn't difficult, your exploits have become the talk of the town. Everybody seems to know where you are to be found."

"Why have you not told of what you know before this?" enquired Holmes.

"I have been very ill. I am, even now, but little improved," she replied.

"Why did you not tell the truth at the trial?" asked Holmes.

"I could not bring myself to do so, I could only say, over and over again that Jim was innocent. I could not bear the shame which would, inevitably, have come to me and my family, if I had told the whole truth.

"My statement was not enough to save Jim, and I was in such a bad way at the time, that I did not make a very convincing witness. I never intended any harm to come to Jim. Little did I know where my lies would lead, when I gave my false account the morning after the supposed attack. But somehow, after I had given it, I could not go back upon it, no matter what followed, until now."

Tears began to roll down her ravaged face. "I am so sorry, so sorry," said she, and her voice rose almost to a shriek.

I patted her on her shoulder, in an attempt to comfort her.

"Perhaps you would like to rest for a while, before you go on," I suggested.

She shook her head. "I am so afraid that I might die, or be otherwise unable to tell my story," she said, "that I feel I must tell it now, or perhaps never."

"You shall not die," I said. But I was not wholly convinced of the truth of this.

"You are a kind man, for saying that," she said, "but in any case, I am now prepared to give my true account to you both."

And so we settled down to listen to the young woman's extraordinary story. "As you probably know, Jim and I were childhood sweethearts, and it is mainly because of my father's regard for him, before these terrible events took place, that he allowed me to come and speak to you. After you left yesterday, he became full of doubts about what had happened, we talked, and I told him what I am about to tell you. His desire to see justice done for Jim overcame his fears for me, and he could see that any vilification of me meant nothing to me, if I could put right that which is now so wrong.

"As I say, Jim and I were sweethearts, and considered so right for each other, that it became a common belief that we would, one day, be married. Then, about eighteen months ago, Dick came into my life. He was so very different to Jim, whom

I had already begun to consider uninteresting and dull. I wish, with all my heart, that I had never met Dick!

"My father took against Dick from the beginning, he forbade me to go on seeing him. He had heard of him and knew what he was like. But, because I was out and about on my own so frequently, driving cabs and carriages, I found it easy to steal some time with him.

"My father had said that if I continued my relationship with Dick, he would turn me out of the house and disown me. He said that over his dead body would he see someone like Dick endowed with all my worldly goods and chattels. Life with my father had never been easy, but when Dick came into my life, it became almost impossibly hard, and so I lied to him for peace, and because I was terrified of him.

"Anyway, I was out in the chaise, on the evening of that fateful day, when word reached me that my father had found out that I was still seeing Dick, careful though we had been to keep our trysts a secret, and that he was waiting for me, to confront me with the fact that I had disobeyed him, and probably worse.

"It was with a heavy heart that I went about my duties after hearing such dismal news, but by the time night fell, I had conceived a scheme which might save me, I was not to know at what cost. After I had conveyed my last fare, I drove to a lonely spot about half a mile from the house, released the horse, took possession of the money bag and placed it some distance away. Afterwards, I took off one of the candle lamps, tipped the chaise on to its side, and, using the lamp, set fire to it, I then put the lamp back on its bracket.

"Then I tore my clothes, scratched my face and neck, and rolled in the wet grass and mud: it was pouring with rain at the time. Having retrieved the bag of money, I set off across the fields to the Blue Posts. Although it was dark, I knew the way like the back of my hand. A few hundred yards from the scene of the supposed attack, in the middle of a field, is a small copse; there I buried the money, and continued on my journey.

"I meant to leave the money there for only a short time. I intended to come back after a few weeks to retrieve it and dispose of it where no-one would ever find it. Events, however, overtook me, and I was unable to carry out my resolution.

"When I got to the Blue Posts my appearance caused consternation. Soon after I arrived I had a buzzing in my head and fell into a dead faint, which was quite genuine. Whether this was caused by my exertions or whether it was because of the stress I had been under, since I got the news that my father had found out about Dick, I know not. I think it was both. The next morning, after a troubled night, I gave my false account of what had occurred. Later that day, when I was told that Jim had been arrested for the attack upon me, I became hysterical, my health rapidly declined, and it has never recovered."

"Have you seen Dick Knight since the night of the supposed attack?" asked Holmes.

"No, sir, I have not. Once this terrible story became public, he distanced himself from me, blackguard that he is, and never once asked after me, or came to see how I was faring, not that my father would have made him welcome."

Some colour came into her blanched face as she said this. "I must say, that in some quarters, his refusal to acknowledge that we were once lovers has caused suspicion to fall upon him, and he has, on more than one occasion, been subjected to abuse - which serves him right.

"Jim's cousin, in particular, has steadfastly maintained that he was my assailant, and that I have been shielding him, out of my love for him, which is simply not true. I hope one day to make my apologies to the Broadbent family, in the hope that they will understand the predicament in which I found myself at that time."

I hoped fervently that the Broadbent family would forgive her, but I had profound doubts about the matter.

That, in any case, seemed to be the end of the interview, Polly rose painfully to her feet, and told us that she was going to the police, to tell her story, and asked us to accompany her, to tell of our part in the affair.

When we got back to the hotel, we lunched, and over lunch, Holmes announced that he intended to take the early evening train back to London. I protested at this, but to no avail, and we found ourselves back at Baker Street that night.

Some months had passed after our holiday on the south coast, which had proved to be no holiday at all, when one morning, Holmes, who had been perusing *The Times* after breakfast, wreathed in smoke from his pipe, silently handed me the paper, which he had folded in such a way that the article which he wanted me to see was obvious.

'SUSSEX MAN FREED', was the article's heading. 'Mr. James Broadbent, (it went on) who was imprisoned more than a year ago for the vicious and cowardly attack upon a young woman cab driver, was yesterday released following an official enquiry, in which the celebrated detective Mr. Sherlock Holmes played no small part. It was he, with his colleague Dr. J. Watson, who found, by means of a tracking dog, a leather bag of money, which had allegedly been stolen by the above named assailant.

Mr. Holmes and his associate confronted the victim of the alleged attack with this evidence, which resulted in a confession on the part of the young woman, Miss Polly Winthrop, that her account of the events of that night had been a complete falsehood. The reasons for her fabricated account are too complex to go into here.

The news of the complete exoneration of Broadbent, together with his being reunited with his family last night, gave rise to scenes of considerable jubilation in his the home town.

The fate of the unhappy woman is not known at this time.'

I smiled and nodded, and handed the paper back to Holmes, who lost no time in cutting out the article with scissors, afterwards pasting it into one of his dusty tomes.

Only Holmes and I knew of the efforts he had put into persuading the authorities to examine the case of Broadbent, efforts which involved some of the highest in the land, and which were only accomplished through the good offices of his brother Mycroft.

"I confess, Watson," he said, when he had sat back down and lit another pipe, "that I derive more pleasure from the release of someone wrongfully accused of a crime, than I do when my work results in the imprisonment of a wrongdoer."

The Adventure of the Admiral

It was a gloomy early morning in October and Holmes was sitting in an armchair in front of the recently lit fire. The floor around him was littered with newspapers, for which he had sent as soon as he arose. He was smoking his third pipe of the day, and was drumming his fingers, with impatience, on the arm of the chair. The previous evening had seen the appearance of Lestrade. He had told us the story which now formed the headlines of most of the morning papers. Holmes had devoured these accounts, one after the other, and then allowed the papers to fall upon the floor without so much as glancing at the rest of the news of the day.

Just then the newsagent's boy for whose arrival he had been waiting, entered with another armful of papers, and Holmes, having tipped him and sent him on his way, began the process once again.

The previous evening, just as we were dressing for dinner, Lestrade had burst into our apartments like a thunderbolt. He had been beside himself with excitement, gibbering incoherently, and it had taken the combined efforts of both of us to calm him down sufficiently to make sense of what he was trying to tell us. He had just come from a bank in Bond Street, the premises of Ephgrave and Company, where there had been a most extraordinary robbery.

What he told us about the scene in the bank defied belief. It seemed that, at about six-thirty, a patrolling constable was walking past the doors, which had been closed but not locked, when he had heard a great commotion issuing from within. After he had glanced inside, he had summoned help with his whistle before investigating further. It turned out that this course of events was most fortuitous. Lestrade had been summoned from a coffee shop where he habitually took refreshment at that time of day, by one of the constables who had been summoned to the bank. Lestrade and the constable eventually reached the bank and, joined by several other constables, they made their way inside. What they found there was chaos, pure and simple.

The elderly chairman of the bank was sitting on the floor, bawling and cheering as his wife, an elderly and normally dignified lady, danced, in a frenzied fashion, around the floor of the banking hall with one member of staff after another, while most of those not dancing stood around convulsed by fits of laughter, as if this was the funniest thing in the world. The constable who had been the first to arrive at the bank, was watching the proceedings, also doubled up with laughter. He was standing, helmetless, in a mock-threatening manner, brandishing his truncheon and scribbling in his notebook. These scribblings were subsequently found to be mostly nonsense, although they had begun in a completely normal fashion, and had afterwards rapidly deteriorated.

Two members of staff were kicking his helmet around the banking hall, as if taking part in an impromptu game of football. Two or three members of staff were lying, insensible, upon the floor, while another sat crying hysterically, tearing sheet after sheet of paper to pieces.

In one of the side walls was a large hole, leading to the premises next door, below it lay a pile of masonry and plaster. There was no trace of any money, except for coins of small denomination. The cash boxes and drawers were empty, as was the safe, whose door stood wide open.

Lestrade told us that he had stood, open-mouthed and irresolute, when he saw the gaping hole and the antics of the bank staff, while the constables waited for his orders. After a minute or two had passed, he had been struck by the ludicrousness of the scene, and had begun to smile broadly.

One of the constables, after seeing the smile on the lips of his superior, had uttered a loud guffaw, and this had had the effect of jolting Lestrade into action. He had realised that there was something wrong with the atmosphere of the bank, and he got the constables outside where a crowd was beginning to gather. Although his mind was clouded by the influence of some unknown agent, he managed to dispatch one of the constables to Charing Cross Hospital, for medical help, and he supervised the dispersal of the crowd. The hospital sent two ambulances, and the bank was quickly evacuated, although some of the staff complained bitterly at being so disturbed as if they were children at play.

The bank was made secure for the night, and two constables were posted to keep watch, one in the street, and the other in the alley which ran behind the premises. Once all these arrangements were made, Lestrade had called upon us.

As soon as Holmes had heard this strange narrative, he was all for going down to the bank that instant, but Lestrade was firm in his resolve not to allow anyone inside until the next morning. Holmes had, rather sulkily, accepted this dictum, and he arranged to meet Lestrade at the doors of the bank at eight.

By half past seven Holmes had finished reading the accounts of the robbery in the latest batch of newspapers, and he now sat silently with his last pipe, long grown cold, in his hand.

We had had the story, in some detail, from Lestrade the night before, and I could not determine why he had perused the newspaper accounts with such avidity. When he finally roused himself from his deliberations, and enquired what time it was, I felt that it was safe to ask why he had so diligently scrutinised the accounts of the robbery.

"I wanted to make certain that there had not been an early explanation of the case," said he. He left it for me to decide whether he was for or against such an event.

Shortly after this, we took a cab to Bond Street, where we found Lestrade outside the bank, together with an elderly man, and two middle-aged men. A constable stood to one side. When we were introduced, we discovered that the elderly man was Lord Ephgrave, the owner of the bank. This was the man who, the previous evening, had found it so amusing to watch his wife dancing with such abandon. The other men were two of the directors of the bank.

Lord Ephgrave did not seem amused now, and he had a tendency to avoid the eye of everybody present.

Keys were produced, and we all went inside. Holmes gave a cursory glance at the disarray which we found there, and made a bee-line for the hole in the wall. Lestrade, who seemed to be as subdued as the chairman, accompanied him. Lord Ephgrave and the directors repaired to his office, where they bent themselves to the task of determining how much money had been stolen.

Holmes and Lestrade clambered through the hole, and went into the building next door which had been the emporium of a bespoke tailor, but was now unoccupied. After some hesitation, I went after them.

As soon as I climbed through the hole, which was about three feet square, Holmes issued a curt injunction that I remain where I was. He was examining the tracks of some kind of cart or other wheeled vehicle, which had been left in the dust caused by the making of the hole. The tracks led to the rear of the premises. There were ample traces of many foot-prints in the dust caused by the making of the hole, as if a number of persons had walked up and down.

There were signs that those persons had spent some considerable time in this place, because there were empty beer-bottles, sandwich wrappings, apple cores, and similar debris scattered around.

"Three men have been here," declared Holmes, "judging by the marks of different foot-wear in the dust, and they used a two-wheeled hand-cart of some kind to carry a considerable load to the place where the wall has been pierced."

A ladder stood against the wall which had been breached, near the top of which was a small hole. Holmes climbed up the ladder with a long strip of cloth of the kind used for hat-bands, which he had found. As Lestrade and I gazed up at him, he fed the strip through the hole, until only a short length protruded on our side of the wall. He then climbed down and went back into the bank. Lestrade and I climbed through the hole to join him.

He was gazing up at a place next to the ceiling, where the strip of cloth hung down like a banner. The hole on this side was disguised by an egg-and-tongue frieze which ran around all four walls of the banking-hall next to the ceiling, and also by the shadow in which it lay, despite the fact that all the gas-lights had by now been lit.

"Very nice," said Lestrade, scratching his head, "but I don't see where it gets us."

Holmes smiled enigmatically at him, went back through the hole in the wall, and we dutifully followed him.

Holmes went down the passage which led to the rear of the premises. Here, in a spacious room fitted with a large number of shelves, now empty, stood the hand-cart. This room had obviously been the stock-room of the former tailor. A double door led to a yard outside, as could be seen through a grimy, barred window. The hand-cart bore the name of the tailor, and was of a common type, having two large, iron wheels at one end, and two legs at the end with the handles.

Holmes examined the cart, and found, in one of the corners, a piece of thick-walled, black rubber tubing about three inches long and about an inch in diameter. A split ran along most of its length.

"I commend this piece of tubing to your attention," said Holmes, to Lestrade, "it is of the utmost significance, for its presence provides a solution to the curious behaviour of the bank staff yesterday evening." Lestrade's response to this was a puzzled frown, and a nervous shake of the head, which seemed, almost, to be an involuntary reaction.

Because Lestrade had shown so little interest in it, my friend placed the piece of rubber tube in his overcoat pocket saying, as he did so, that he would take good care of it.

Holmes now opened the double doors, which proved not to be fastened in any way even though they had heavy bolts, and we went out into the yard. A broken padlock lay on the flagstones of the yard, near the doors. At one side of the yard, which had high walls, was a pile of refuse, consisting of cardboard boxes of scraps of cloth and other rubbish, which had collapsed and burst open due to rain. There were also a few empty wooden crates. The yard had an unkempt appearance, and weeds grew between the flagstones, which showed, by way of hoof prints and wheel tracks, that a large horse-drawn vehicle of some kind, had been in use there, recently. The tracks led to a pair of tall gates at the bottom of the yard.

We, all three, strolled down the yard to the gates at the far end. When Lestrade opened one of them, a constable, who was standing in the alley which ran down behind the yards of the various shops, stiffened to attention, and saluted. Lestrade nodded to him, and we went back down the yard, and into the stock-room.

When we had arrived back at the site of the hole, Holmes announced that he had seen enough, and that he was now going back to Baker Street. Lestrade shrugged his shoulders, he was well versed in Holmes's peculiar ways, after his many dealings with him, and he bade us good-day as we scrambled back through the hole.

When we found ourselves back in the street outside the bank, Holmes crossed to the other side and walked up and down the pavement, for some distance, gazing up at the façades of the buildings behind me. He was observed doing so by the rather bemused constable, and my equally bemused self.

It had become a fine day with watery sunshine, and after Holmes rejoined me on my side of the street, he announced that he intended to walk back to our lodgings. He called at Bradley's on the way down Oxford Street, and purchased a pound of strong tobacco. When we got back to our rooms, Holmes made himself comfortable in an armchair before the fire with his pipe. I was still in the dark as to what had occurred at the bank and, in particular, I could not understand why a small piece of rubber tube had so held the interest of my friend and why he considered it to be the key to the peculiar antics of the bank staff the previous evening. I proceeded to voice these thoughts aloud.

"There is no mystery about any of this," said my friend. "It is as clear as day to me. However, for your benefit, I shall summarise the various facts. It is obvious, now, that the robbery had been carefully planned for some time. This particular bank was selected by the gang, precisely because the premises next door were vacant. The only real risk, once they had entered those premises, was their first task: the boring of the small hole, near the ceiling. It was risky because they had no way of knowing for certain that the hole would not be discovered before they were ready to use it. No matter how careful they were in making that little hole, some dust and particles of masonry must have fallen to the floor of the bank. They simply had to trust to luck that this debris would not arouse suspicion of any kind. Luck proved to be on their side, and it went unnoticed or, at least, an explanation for it was found which did not lead to the discovery of the hole. A thing which aided them was the fact that the bank and the premises of the former tailor were two of six contiguous buildings which had been constructed at the same time, as may be easily be determined by observing the identical façades of all six."

"How did this aid them?"

"Because it meant that the ceiling of the bank was at the same height as the ceiling of the vacant premises, and so they were able to bore the hole in exactly the right place."

"What part does the piece of rubber tube play in the strange behaviour of the bank staff?" I enquired, unable to keep my curiosity in check any longer.

Holmes chuckled, and asked what I knew of nitrous oxide.

"Nitrous oxide is used as an anaesthetic, especially with regard to dentistry. I have been present, once or twice, at minor operations when it was used, supplied from an iron reservoir. It is mainly used in minor operations of short duration." I paused, and was about to ask him why he had asked me about that particular gas and then I understood. "You mean that they had a supply of nitrous oxide on their side of the wall, which they conveyed to the atmosphere of the bank by means of a rubber tube pushed through the small hole."

"Bravo, Watson," said Holmes, obviously delighted by my correct interpretation of the facts. "I suppose, by the way, that you could not recall the name of the firm which supplied the nitrous oxide used during the operations which you mentioned?"

"I am sorry, but it seems to have slipped my mind," I replied, after thinking hard for a time.

"No matter, it will be an easy thing to discover."

"Would they not have needed a fairly large volume to produce the effects which Lestrade described in such graphic detail?" said I, steering the conversation back to the main theme.

"Since those effects were produced, we must conclude that they did indeed have a large supply at their disposal, probably in liquid form, in wrought-iron reservoirs of some sort. The gas is, in fact, one of the easiest to liquefy. The sequence of events is clear. Once they had gained access to the empty premises, they made the small hole, during a time when the bank was empty of personnel. After that was achieved, they waited for a few days, to make certain that they were safe. Then they brought their supply of nitrous oxide to the vacant building, under cover of darkness, in all probability. They then remained in the empty premises all night, and most of the next day, because they could not begin their task until the bank was closed to the public at four o'clock.

"Soon after that time, they brought their supply of gas to a point below the small hole, using that hand-cart, and began the process of introducing it into the atmosphere of the bank. When they were satisfied that enough had been used, and that the persons in the bank were all unconscious, they removed their supply to a conveyance of some kind, which was waiting in the yard beyond the stock-room doors. They then broke through the wall and removed all the cash that they could find, loaded it into the conveyance, and left before the alarm was raised."

"How could they be sure that everyone present was unconscious?"

"The simple answer to that is that they could not. However, nitrous oxide has another property besides that of producing anaesthesia: it causes the rational, judgmental part of the mind to become suspended, even in admixture with a quantity of air. This causes, in some few cases, a tendency to find even the most commonplace events hysterically funny, and gives rise to its other, more common, name: laughing gas, which is some-thing of a misnomer, because, as I have said, it does not generally have that effect. In this case, however, it does seem to have lived up to the name by which it is usually termed, perhaps because it was administered *en masse*, and one person laughing set the others off. The effect of suspending reason in all persons inhaling it is universal and so, even if one or more of the bank personnel were still conscious when the gang broke through the wall, they would not have been able to make sense of what was going on. This property of the gas also explains why no-one present in the bank was capable of raising an early alarm. By the time the effects began to be manifest, it would already have been too late for rational action. The effects were beginning to wear off by the time the police intervened. I think, however, that Lestrade was suffering, just a trifle, from the effects when he came to us with the news." Holmes smiled after he spoke these last few words.

"How do you know so much about the physiological properties of nitrous oxide?" I asked, genuinely puzzled. "I am a doctor, but much of what you have said was unknown to me."

"Clearly, you have not read Humphry Davy's researches on the inspiration of nitrous oxide, published almost a hundred years ago, and which gave rise to similar experiments by many other notable men."

"No. I must admit that I have not."

"It is a fascinating study, which I can thoroughly recommend. He said, among other things, that trying to describe the effects was rather like blind men using the language of sight."

I felt that we were straying too far from the matter in hand, and so I asked Holmes why the small hole, through which the gas was introduced, was made near the ceiling.

"The reason why the initial hole was made near the ceiling, was mainly for the purposes of concealment, but it served another purpose as well. Nitrous oxide has a density markedly greater than that of air. It is in fact, more than one and a half times as dense as air. Therefore it had a greater chance to mix uniformly with the atmosphere of the bank, as it moved down through it, than would have been the case if it had been introduced, say, at floor level, where it might have formed a layer. The persons who used it must have been fully aware of its physical, as well as physiological, properties."

"When the gang broke through the wall, why was it that they did not succumb to its effects?"

"I do not know the answer to that, but I am certain that they must have evolved some method to ensure that that did not occur."

Just then we both heard the ring of our bell, and a few moments later, Lestrade was shown into our apartment by Mrs. Hudson.

"I have just come from the hospital, where the bank staff were treated last evening," he announced, after a nod to us both. "The doctors there said that they had all been exposed to..."

"Nitrous oxide," said my friend, finishing his sentence.

"Why, that is exactly what they told me," he said in a hushed, wondering tone. "But how did you know that?"

"The bank robbers introduced nitrous oxide into the bank from the premises next door by means of a rubber tube. I shall explain the method used more fully later," said Holmes. "Was there anything else?"

"Yes," said Lestrade, still somewhat astonished, "but the doctors dismissed it as the ravings of someone under the influence of the gas, coming as it did in the middle of a hodge-podge of disordered thoughts and impressions. The person who uttered these nonsensical ramblings, one of the clerks, was clearly very much under the influence at that time, and could recall little or nothing of what he had said, when the effects of the gas wore off."

"Nevertheless," said my friend, "I would be glad to hear it."

Lestrade sighed resignedly, removed his hat, and sat heavily down upon a chair. "The clerk said that part of the wall flowed away like water with a noise like a waterfall, and that two large, bespectacled frogs or toads came into the bank. They were wearing brown leather suits covering large humps on their backs and chests, and were carrying sacks. The clerk addressed a few remarks to them, but they ignored him. They walked about making hissing sounds, and they put all the money they could find into the sacks. The clerk was not frightened by them, nor did he think that their sudden appearance, and subsequent actions, were strange or unusual in any way. He simply accepted them, as he accepted the fact that most of his colleagues had become insensible. He believes that he lost consciousness soon afterwards, because he does not remember how he came to be in a hospital ward."

Holmes nodded slowly. "I must say that I had expected something of the sort. We are fortunate that somebody present was sufficiently *compos mentis* to speak of it."

"You don't mean to tell me that you expected two frogs to climb through that hole, and all the rest of it," said Lestrade, incredulously. "I know that you are a clever man, and that you have been of some help to me in the past, but now I think you have gone too far. I simply don't believe that you could have foreseen those events."

"Just before you arrived," said Holmes, imperturbably, "Watson raised the question of how the robbers managed to enter the bank without being overcome by the nitrous oxide which had already subdued the staff. I had dimly conceived of some kind of protective breathing apparatus, and now that I have heard the narrative of the clerk, I can see that I was correct. I could not, of course, have foreseen the form it would take, nor the interpretation of it by someone under the influence of nitrous oxide. I am satisfied, however, that the frog-like appearance of the two men involved was due to the fact that they were wearing such an apparatus. The humps upon their backs and chests, under the leather suits, were occasioned by bladders of some kind, containing sufficient air for them to accomplish their task. The leather hoods covering those bladders also covered their heads, necessitating the incorporation of two glazed holes, which gave the appearance of spectacles, so that they could see. The hissing sounds were made by some kind of valve mechanism, which ensured that they inspired the air in the bladders, and not the air in the bank."

Lestrade and I sat in silence for some time after this pronouncement. I could see the logic of it, although I remained doubtful as to whether my friend had reached the right result.

"I suppose," said Lestrade grudgingly, breaking the silence, "that we will have to accept this explanation, assuming the clerk did see what he said he saw, and was not wandering in his mind."

"Thank you," said Holmes with mock humility.

Lestrade also told us, before he left, that the robbers had taken the sum of just over ninety-four thousand pounds and that they seemed to have disappeared without trace. The bank proposed to offer a reward of five thousand pounds for the return of the money and the capture of the members of the gang.

When we were alone, Holmes filled his pipe, once more, from the supply of tobacco which he had purchased that morning and sat in his fireside armchair. Soon, he was in one of his deeply introspective reveries, and I found myself tiptoeing around him, when I found it necessary to move at all, and I endeavoured to preserve an atmosphere of silence, in order not to disturb his train of thought.

Holmes, after about an hour, jumped up from his chair, put on his hat and coat, and left the room without a word. I followed him to the landing, and called down to him as he reached the foot of the stairs.

"Where are you going?"

"Oxford Street."

The front door banged behind him, and I was left to ponder on the reason for his sudden departure.

I had expected my friend to be gone for some time, and it therefore came as a surprise to me, when he returned within twenty minutes.

"I have been to see my dentist," said he, answering my unasked question, as he doffed his street clothes. "I needed to know which firm supplies nitrous oxide, liquefied in iron bottles or cylinders, to the dental and medical profession. It seems that there is only one such firm in this country: Messrs. Coxeter of London."

"That was the name," said I, nodding. "I remember it now."

Holmes smiled briefly and continued: "In America, the agent for the supply of liquid nitrous oxide cylinders is the S. S. White Company of Utica, but we need not concern ourselves with them just now."

A silence fell, which Holmes broke by asking me whether I had any engagement that evening.

"I have no particular plans," I replied, "Why do you ask?"

"I thought we might dine out this evening, I had in mind that new restaurant in Soho, the Café Madeleine."

"I have heard that is more than a trifle bohemian."

"Yes, so have I, but perhaps just this once..."

We got back quite late. The food and drink at the restaurant had proved to be very good, but the atmosphere had been rather rowdy, and I was glad to be in our quiet lodgings once more.

We smoked our last pipes of the day, and retired for the night.

The next morning, Holmes left for the offices of Messrs. Coxeter, in order to make inquiries, and I had to put in an appearance at my surgery, with the usual round of visits following.

Holmes was not present when I arrived back in the late afternoon, but he came in not long afterwards. He seemed to be in an excellent frame of mind, and I assumed that things had gone well for him. He emerged from his bedroom wearing dressing gown and slippers, and I took this to mean that he did not contemplate going out again that day. After he had seated himself in his favourite chair with his pipe, he proved to be more than ready to recount the events of his day.

"How Lestrade's face fell," he began, laughing.

"When?"

"When I met him coming into Coxeter's offices, as I was leaving. I believe that he thought he had stolen a march on me for once, and he would then have come round here this evening and crowed about it. As it is, I do not think we shall see him for a day or two. I must say, though, that his detective work seems to be improving."

"Did you discover anything of significance?"

"Coxeter's were very helpful, but an hour or two of examining their books did not reveal anything of significance, it would have been a wasted visit, indeed, but for a chance remark made by the general manager, just when I was about to withdraw. He intended it as a joke, but it galvanised me when I heard it."

"What exactly did he say?"

"He told me that sales were up on last year, and that the value of their product was becoming more and more assured. Had he any doubts about it they vanished when a consignment of cylinders and some other equipment, was stolen from the factory about two months ago. Only a few papers reported it, as it was overshadowed by the Cornish tin mine disaster, which all but drove it from the papers. I remember reading of it, but as it seemed of small significance, and because I had other cases on hand, I allowed it to slip from my mind."

"You think there is a connection between the theft of the gas and the bank robbery?"

"It is virtually a certainty."

"How much nitrous oxide was taken?"

"About five hundred pounds in weight."

"Including the weight of containers?"

"No, that is the net weight of the gas."

"That is a very considerable quantity."

"It represents the production of a full month at the factory."

"How much was used at Ephgrave's Bank?"

"That is difficult to tell exactly, but let us see. The banking hall was about twenty feet by twenty feet, by ten feet in height, so, four thousand cubic feet. We do not know the dimensions exactly, but they will be of that order. If we assume a fifty per cent concentration is enough to produce unconsciousness, then they used two thousand cubic feet, which weighed ... "

Here, Holmes made some calculations on his shirt cuff. "About two hundred and thirty pounds, assuming a room temperature of seventy degrees Fahrenheit."

"So, they have enough for another robbery, if they so choose."

"So it would seem, unless we catch them first."

"Were any clues left at the factory?"

"The general manager was kind enough to show me the shed from where the gas was stolen. There had been a forced entry. Before this, the night-watchman had been overpowered and bound and gagged. He came to no harm, but was unable to give a description of his assailants. The whole thing bore the hallmarks of a professional gang. The trail had, of course, long gone cold, and there was little I could do."

Holmes fell silent for some minutes after this, then he said: "There was one other thing which I learned at the Coxeter company."

"What was that?"

"While I was there, I asked to see their entire range of rubber tubing, none that I saw bore any resemblance to the piece which I found at the bank. When I showed it to the general manager, he was of the opinion that it was of a kind used by divers, where air is pumped down from the surface, often under a considerable pressure, to a brass or copper helmet worn by the diver. I can see a vague connection between this fact, and the use of nitrous oxide, and also, yet again, between it and the protective breathing apparatus used by the robbers to ensure that they did not succumb to the effects of the gas."

"I agree. The facts do seem to be related."

Holmes mused for a few moments. "On the morrow, I really must find out whether the tubing, of which I have a sample, is the kind used by divers."

The next morning, Holmes took the piece of tubing to a celebrated London firm which specialised in diving equipment, and was delighted to be told that the tube was unquestionably of their manufacture.

"It does narrow the field of search a little," said Holmes, when we discussed it later that day.

"What will you do now?"

"I have made inquiries, and I have discovered that there are only three wharves in London which cater for diving-vessels, excluding Royal Naval diving-vessels. Two are in Deptford, the other is in Woolwich. I have no doubt that there are public houses which are frequented by divers in both districts. I shall go to those public houses posing as an ex-Royal Navy diver, who is seeking a position."

"Do you know anything about practical diving, Royal Naval or otherwise?"

"Nothing at all," said Holmes, with a shrug of his shoulders, and a hearty, short laugh.

"Then how are you to convince those who have such experience?" I said, concerned. "They would see through you in a moment, and the most dreadful consequences might result. They are not likely to take kindly to an impostor, especially an impostor who asks a lot of questions."

"In the first place," said Holmes, settling himself more comfortably in his chair, and reaching for his pipe and tobacco, "when I go to a public house on a mission of this kind, I do not ask questions, I listen. I have found that once I have put a person at his ease, a facility with which I am blessed, they are only too happy to talk to me, I find that I do not have to say very much beyond an occasional prompt, or comment. There are always those, of course, who wish to draw one out. I shall avoid such people as best I can. I have found that there is a trick one can use to ensure an almost uninterrupted flow of speech from one's conversational partner."

"What is it?"

"It takes a little time to learn the art, but, in essence, it consists of appearing to be less interesting, knowledgeable or accomplished than the person one is having a conversation with." Holmes, having filled his pipe, lit it from the fire with a spill, which he then shook to extinguish.

"I considered this for a few moments, and then I said: "It seems a very simple idea, but I must say that I have never used conversations in the way you do, as a means of eliciting information from an unsuspecting person, rather than simply to pass the time in a pleasant manner."

"I can make conversation in the way you describe, but it is not part of my temperament to do so, especially in a situation such as I have described, where time might be of the essence. I can, by the way, assure you that the reverse of what I have just said is also true, in that if one's partner in conversation realises or suspects that one knows more than they do about the subject, or subjects, discussed, they invariably fall silent, and become on their guard. That way breeds resentment, also."

"And in the second place?" said I, wishing to get back to the matter which concerned me: that of the safety of my friend.

"In the second place, I shall not be entirely ignorant of matters concerning practical diving by this time tomorrow, when I leave for Deptford. I have, by the way, decided to go to Deptford first."

"How so?"

"I have armed myself with an Admiralty volume entitled *The Royal Naval Handbook of Diving*, and I shall spend every waking minute of the next twenty-four hours digesting its contents."

"I see," said I, already feeling much better about my friend's expedition.

Soon after this, Holmes fetched the book to which he had referred, and began to peruse it.

Conversation became impossible, and, as I retired to my room, my last view of Holmes was of him smoking his pipe and reading in the circle of light thrown by a lamp, totally engrossed. He did not look up when I wished him good-night.

The next morning, I was startled to see my friend occupied in exactly the same way as when I last saw him, except that the lamp was no longer lit. The oil in its glass reservoir was considerably depleted.

"Good morning, Watson," said Holmes, glancing in my direction.

"But, my dear fellow," I exclaimed, "you have been up all night."

"Not quite all night. I fell asleep at some point. When I woke it was dawn. I extinguished the lamp and resumed reading at the place where I left off."

Holmes was persuaded, by the combined efforts of Mrs.

Hudson and myself, to eat some breakfast. Soon afterwards, he went back to the book, and finished it by the early afternoon.

At seven, when he was ready to leave, he was wearing a heavy jacket, with a packet of sandwiches wedged in the pocket, a peaked Royal Naval officer's cap, with the insignia removed and the peak deliberately cracked and scratched, stout boots, which had purposely been scuffed and battered, and a blotched and stained pair of trousers. He wore a false, full-set beard to complement his seafaring appearance. At our doorstep I gripped his forearms, and wished him well. He lit his pipe, a short clay, clapped me on the back and I watched him go until he vanished down the gas-lit street.

Some hours later, I was trying, in vain, to distract myself with a novel, but my senses were straining, listening for a key in the lock of our front door or some other sign that my friend had returned. Then I heard a cab, which had been driven in a leisurely way down the almost deserted street, halt outside our door. I looked at my watch, it was just before one. I heard a brief exchange, the front door opened and closed quietly, and then I heard the familiar tread on the stairs.

"Holmes," I cried, surprising myself with the emotion which welled up in me, "I am very glad to see you safe and sound." A strong smell of ale and tobacco reached me a few moments after my friend entered, but his eye was bright, and his carriage erect, and I could tell that he had not imbibed more than he needed to.

"I have much to tell you," said he.

"It will keep until after breakfast, you really must get some sleep. The only important thing, is that you have returned unscathed."

Holmes put up no resistance to my suggestion, and we both retired for the night. The following morning, after breakfast, we settled ourselves in our chairs before the fire with our pipes, and Holmes began to narrate his experiences of the night before.

"When I arrived in Deptford last evening, I discovered that the diving fraternity of both wharves, which I mentioned yesterday, make use of the same tavern: The Ship Aground. It is a noisy, dirty place, and in the comparatively short time I was under its roof there were no fewer than three violent confrontations among the people who frequent the place. The last confrontation, perhaps because the men involved were further into their cups, involved the use of knives. I was not personally involved in any of these altercations, but I had a bad time for a few minutes when the police arrived to break up the knife fight."

"Why was that?"

"The sergeant in charge of the constables was Anderson, a man who knows me by sight. Luckily, my disguise proved impenetrable. Had he recognised me, I would have had to leave the premises with him, for the sake of my safety and my investigation would have been seriously hampered."

"What did you discover?"

"During the course of the evening, I found that there is a man known to seafaring men as The Admiral, whose actual name is Carpenter. Until fairly recently he was a wealthy man, he made most of his money by recovering valuable materials, including gold and silver, from sunken shipwrecks. He specialises in wrecks which are outside the jurisdiction of any particular country, and so avoids any possible trouble from the authorities of any nation. He was formerly the captain of a merchantman, one of a fleet of such ships owned by a London company. One stormy night his ship was lost some fifty miles off the Scillies, he and his second mate were the only survivors. The ship was carrying silver ingots from Argentina.

"There was an enquiry by the company, and Captain Carpenter was found to be negligent, even though the second mate insisted that the captain had done all he could to prevent the disaster.   Carpenter was removed from the employ of the company, and found it impossible to find work elsewhere. After some time had elapsed, he and the second mate resolved to recover the silver from the wreck, and they managed to scrape together sufficient money to charter a vessel and pay divers to do so. Captain Carpenter had the rough position of the site of the wreck, which was eventually found, lying in about twelve fathoms of water.   The expedition was successful, others followed, and Carpenter's new career began. From time to time bad luck forced Carpenter and his men to tackle rather more dubious work, including smuggling and gun-running. All these activities went well for him until the ship, which he had managed to purchase, was wrecked in the severe weather of last March. This time the whole crew escaped with their lives, but Carpenter was left virtually penniless.   He is, however, an intelligent, clever and very resourceful man, with many interests, besides being well-read in the natural sciences, and I have reason to believe that he soon found a way out of his difficulty."

"I take it that you met him last night?"

"Indeed I did not," said Holmes, laughing.   "He is a shadowy, almost legendary figure, he does not normally involve himself, except at a distance, with any land-based concern. I had this story from one who had served under him, a man who admires him, and would be only too glad to put sea under his command, when he gets together the money to buy another ship, and equip it appropriately." Here Holmes paused, giving me, as he did so, a significant look.

"Are you saying that this man Carpenter is behind the bank robbery?"

"I have not sufficient information to be able to say that, but last night I gleaned certain indications.   Indications whose significance would have no meaning to anyone who was not already familiar with the facts concerning the robbery. Not the least of these is the revelation that Carpenter has recently come into a great deal of money and has bought a ship which is being fitted out at Deptford diving-wharf. She will be ready to sail within a month. I have been promised a place upon it, as third diver, and to that end, I am to see Captain Carpenter this evening at his town-house in Chelsea, at eight."

"Shall you go?"

"I most assuredly shall."

"Is it not a dangerous errand?"

Holmes considered for a few moments, and I could see that he was weighing doubts and certainties in his mind.

"I think there is a risk only if I am discovered to be an impostor," he said, at last. "In any case, I have to go, because I do not know for certain that he is our man. I hope to gather enough information to-night, both verbal and by observation, to remove all doubts."

Holmes spent much of the day refreshing his memory upon certain points in the *Handbook*.

Then, when the time for his appointment drew near, he applied himself, meticulously, to the application of the disguise he had used the previous evening. This had only just been completed to his satisfaction, when Mrs. Hudson showed Lestrade up to our rooms, before either of us could intervene to stop her. She left without taking any particular notice of Holmes, now fully disguised.

"Halloa!" said Lestrade, on seeing my companion, "and who might this cove be?"

There was an awkward pause, during which I contained my mirth with difficulty. I simply had no idea how my friend would react. Lestrade looked quizzically at me and then at my friend, obviously somewhat put out that no-one saw fit to enlighten him. Holmes had obviously chosen not to give anything away, because he drew himself to his full height, and saluted Lestrade in a servile manner. "Leading Seaman Rodney Nelson, at your service, sir," he said, in a strong West Country accent.

"Come to see Mr. Holmes, have you?"

"Yes, sir. Been waiting over an hour now, sir."

"I wish you luck, Holmes is a difficult man to pin down. I came to see him myself, but if he is not here, I cannot stay."

This last filled me with relief, for I was totally unprepared for a lengthy deception

"No relation to Horatio, I suppose?" said Lestrade, as he left, smiling at his ready wit.

"Distant, sir, very distant."

"Well, I'll leave you to it."

I was just able to wait until I heard our front door slam before I burst out laughing. So overcome was I that I had to sit down. Holmes grinned broadly at me through his beard, and then he too, started to laugh.

"Really, Holmes," I said, when we had recovered our composure, "I do not know, for the life of me, why you did it."

"It was a heaven-sent opportunity to put my disguise to the test," said he, archly.

This provoked another squall of laughter from us both.

"Needless to say," he continued, "the false papers which I took the opportunity of obtaining while I was at the Admiralty, are for a man with a somewhat more prosaic name than that which I gave Lestrade. I am to assume the identity of a man who really exists. His name is William Hanson, and he was a Royal Navy diver until about a year ago, when he was forced to temporarily stand down from active service, due to an injury, and is at present recuperating in his cottage on the south coast. He has given his blessing to the deception, and has promised to keep low until this business has been cleared up."

We were in the best of humour, until Holmes left to keep his appointment. In fact, it was only after he had been gone for some time, that my misgivings regarding his safety returned.

For the second time in twenty-four hours, I was alone and beset by the knowledge that my friend was out on a dangerous mission. This time, however, I decided not to remain indoors. I put on my hat and coat and went out into the town. I had no particular object, and wandered aimlessly about, looking into the brightly-lit shop windows in Regent Street and Oxford Street.

In my mind's eye I purchased suits of clothing, pipes, boxes of chocolate, umbrellas, and a number of other items, until I felt like the Walrus in *Through The Looking Glass*, who talked of many things, including cabbages and kings. Later, I found myself in Shaftesbury Avenue, where I was tempted to go into a theatre, but I decided against it and slowly made my way home.

When I got back to our lodgings, there was no sign of Holmes, although it was past ten. I sat in an armchair before the dwindling fire and smoked a pipe. I must have nodded off, because the next thing I knew was that I was waking from a terrible nightmare, which involved the death of my friend. In my confusion, I had no idea how long I had been asleep. But when I looked at my watch, it was twenty minutes to six. I sprang to my feet in considerable agitation, something had clearly gone wrong with the plans of my friend.

I paced up and down, trying to gather my wits. My first thought was to go to Lestrade, in order to acquaint him with the facts of the matter. But something seemed to tell me that Holmes was not at Carpenter's house, nor would any evidence be found that he had ever been there, a man like Carpenter would be far too careful for that to be the case. It was unlikely, for the same reason, that any evidence to connect him with the bank robbery would be found there, if Holmes's assumptions that he had master-minded it were correct.

If Lestrade and I were to go down to the house in Chelsea, accompanied by constables, the police would be able to do nothing, and if Holmes was a prisoner elsewhere, assuming he was still alive, the result would be his inevitable death at the hands of his captors, the minions of Carpenter. All traces of the crime would be removed, including the body of my friend, and his disappearance would be unresolved for all time.

I finished pacing, and stood there, irresolute, for some time, trying to conjecture what my friend would do, if he were in my shoes. One thing was certain, he would act alone. This, then, was what I must do, if ever I were to see Holmes alive. The thought that he might already be dead, as in that terrible dream, brought a moistness to my eyes and a tightness to my throat. But I shook off this notion with some difficulty, and tried, instead, to evolve a plan of action.

Despite the fact that I did not really believe my friend to be there, I nurtured a hope that I might see some sign of him at the address in Chelsea. What else could I do but go there? I did not intend to beard Carpenter in his lair. Rather, I would keep his house under observation, just as Holmes would have done in the same situation. If nothing came of this by noon, at latest, I would have no alternative but to tell Lestrade all that I knew.

I scribbled a note, setting out the facts which Holmes had gleaned about the robbery, and his suspicions regarding Carpenter, together with his address, and added a post-script to the effect that my last action was to go to there. I placed it in an envelope, sealed it, and gave it into the keeping of Mrs. Hudson, with the instruction that she should give it to Lestrade and no other, in the event that I did not return by late evening.

As I stood in the street trying to hail a cab, it was just beginning to get light outside, and the eastern sky showed itself in hues of orange and yellow, with dark striations of clouds.

Around me London was waking, sleepy people trudged past me, news-vendors shouted the headlines, carriages and other vehicles rattled past, and a cheery milkman was whistling as he ladled milk from his churn into the jug of a kitchen maid who stood shivering in the morning chill. Finally I secured a cab to begin my journey to Chelsea.

I told the cabby to stop at the end of the street wherein was Carpenter's house and, after the cab had gone, I walked slowly up the pavement, filling my pipe as I did so. I stopped to light up when I reached the house and gave it a covert glance out of the corner of my eye, then walked on, my heart beating more quickly than my exertions, thus far, seemed to demand.

There had been no activity at the house, save a light burning in a room at ground level, to the right of the front door. There was some shiny, metal object standing just beyond the glass, and the rear wall was fitted with shelves which were filled with books. I do not know what I had expected to see, but I felt a sense of profound disappointment. The terraced house was very ordinary, double-fronted, with bay windows on the ground floor, and of three storeys. It was enclosed at the front by iron railings, and seemed in a good state of repair. I reached the end of the street, and turned left down an alley. After walking down the alley a little distance, I could see that the houses on this side of the street had gardens running down to the river.

I reached the water's edge, and turned left, again, into a narrow, muddy path which ran along the bottom of the gardens. At a point which I judged to be directly at the rear of Carpenter's house, a landing-stage, of which there were several along this part of the river-bank, jutted out a short distance above the river. Nailed to it was a sign bearing the name of Carpenter.

It was high tide, and a grubby, wide-bellied boat stood tied up there, rolling slightly, its chimney smoking. It had obviously just arrived, or was about to leave.

There seemed to be no-one about, but I could not linger at this place, for fear of being observed, and so I went on my way.

I had covered about fifty yards, when I heard voices behind me. I turned to see two men on Carpenter's landing-stage, shouting directions to one another as they cast off. The boat began to steam up the river, away from me. It then turned in mid-stream, and headed down river.

I took advantage of the interval caused by the turning of the boat to walk to the end of another landing stage, which I had just reached. As the boat drew nearer, it was forced to pull in closer to my side of the river to avoid some barges, which were being towed upstream. As it passed me, I caught a glimpse of something partly covered by canvas in the open hold behind the steering cabin, it was a metal cylinder, which bore white lettering. I could only see part of a word: COX-, the rest being covered. Even without the wording, I could see that it was a nitrous oxide cylinder.

I stood stock-still as the boat gathered speed and disappeared down river. Holmes's suspicions had been justified.

As I stood there, it struck me that this activity, so early in the morning, was not unconnected with my friend's visit the previous evening - they were now covering their tracks. I could only assume that this was very bad news for Holmes, my fears for him were renewed, and once again I had to struggle to keep my mind on the present situation.

The boat, although old and battered, had had a freshly painted name at the bows: *Matilda*. It was just possible that this was also the name of Carpenter's new ship. Holmes had not mentioned the name, of that I was certain.

I resolved to go to Deptford to make enquiries about the *Matilda*. Even if I was wrong, I could, at the very least, find out which ship used the boat I had seen as a tender.

I regained the main road, and after a rather lengthy wait for a cab, I started out for the docks. When I reached the diving-wharf at Deptford, which I had found by making a few discreet enquiries, the tide was beginning to ebb, and large numbers of vessels were sailing down the river. Although the weather was chilly, the smell of fish was prevalent, mixed with the smells of tar, coal-smoke, and the sea. This quay, although one of the quieter ones in the port, was still very busy. I felt very out of place as I strolled along it, but I attracted few curious glances.

I then had a piece of good-fortune. There, tied up to the side of a three-masted sailing ship, on the far side of the dock, was the *Matilda*. The ship bore the same name.

Neither ship nor tender showed any sign of life, as I looked across the stretch of water, and I walked around to the landward side of her larger namesake. It was strangely quiet in this corner of the quay. The gang-plank of the ship was in place, and there was no-one nearby.

On an impulse, I ran up the gang-plank, keeping my hand on my service revolver, which was in my overcoat pocket, as I did so. Once on deck, I looked around for a hatch which led below. I found one at last, and in my haste, I tried to climb down the companion-ladder facing away from it, as if it was a flight of stairs. The inevitable result was that I stumbled and fell the last few feet on to the floor below. My fall caused a considerable amount of noise, and I had bruised my ankle so badly that I was forced to limp down the narrow corridor, where I now found myself. Luck seemed to be with me, once more, for I detected no sign that anyone had heard me.

As I neared the end of the corridor, which had doors leading to cabins right and left, I heard a sound too loud to have been caused by rats. It came from the last cabin, which, like the others, had a circular ventilation grid in the door at eye level.

I looked through this and, in the small cabin beyond, lit by a smoky, dim lamp, I saw a heavily bound and gagged man sitting on the floor, huddled against the far wall. There was no mistaking that angular face, even in the poor light of the cabin.

It was Holmes, and the faint gleam of his eyes showed that he was awake. I tried the door, softly. It was locked.

"Holmes," I hissed, in a stage-whisper, through the grid.

The features of my friend had changed to an expression of alertness, and the gleam of reflected light from the eyes seemed to have increased when next I observed them.

Holmes turned his head to my left, and several times nodded, vigorously. He seemed to be trying to tell me something, and I looked in the direction he had indicated, there was nothing to be seen but the door at the end of the corridor. I cautiously opened this and found myself on the threshold of some kind of store-room, with ropes, barrels, and other seafaring gear. My attention, however, was drawn to a number of cylinders of nitrous oxide, a coil of black rubber tubing, and two leather outfits with glass eye-pieces set in the hoods. Then I saw a shallow, glass-fronted cabinet on the wall, the rear panel of which was fitted with several numbered hooks which had keys hanging upon them. I removed the one hanging from the hook numbered five, which was the number on the door of the cabin in which my friend was imprisoned.

Closing the store-room door behind me, I tried the key in the door of Holmes's cabin, it proved to be the right one, and I entered. Kneeling down in the gloom, I removed the gag from his mouth.

"I would dearly like to know how you found me," said Holmes, as soon as he was able to speak, "but this is no time for explanations. You must leave here at once, they will be back at any minute."

"I am not leaving without you!"

"You will not be able to free me in time, you must, instead, fetch Lestrade, the ship sails within the hour."

I picked up the lamp, and held it so that I could see how my friend was bound. He was fastened to a stout ring set in the wall of the ship by means of a length of chain, wrapped several times around his waist and secured by two padlocks. With a heavy heart, I set the lamp down where I had found it.

"There is no-one on board," he continued, "because my appearance has caused something of a panic, and every hand is ashore getting the necessary supplies for the voyage which was not due to take place for three weeks at least. You must replace my gag, and lock the door. Be careful to return the key to the place where you found it, there must be nothing to arouse any suspicion that someone has been here."

"What did they plan to do with you?"

"They were going to wait until they had sailed into deep water, and there they would have thrown me, suitably weighted, overboard, together with all evidence of the bank robbery."

This revelation, so calmly spoken, brought chill to my heart.

"I have my service revolver with me," said I, still considerably shaken, "shall I leave it with you, just in case?"

"It is too risky. If it was discovered, they would probably use it on me. You really must go - now!"

I replaced the gag and performed the other offices which my friend had mentioned. As I made my way back down the corridor, my injured foot, which I had forgotten completely in the few minutes I had passed with my friend, began to hurt very much. I realised that if I was discovered before I left the ship, I would be unable to make a bolt for freedom.

I had, with some difficulty, made my way to the top of the companion-ladder, when I heard the unmistakable sounds of some of the crew returning. I dodged around the side of a deck-house, in time to see three men, heavily laden with sacks, and other supplies, coming up the gang-plank. They did not see me, and they went down the deck towards the stern.

As soon as they were out of sight, and I had made certain that nobody else was going to come aboard, I went to the head of the gang-plank and made my way down it, limping and grimacing with pain. A cart stood on the quay, with a considerable number of sacks, barrels and boxes upon it. The carter sat dozing in his seat, the reins still in his hands. He did not see me, and I, slowly, because of the pain, walked away from the ship. As I got to the head of the quay, two more carts and a carriage could be seen approaching, I hid behind a pile of bales, and they swept past me.

I caught a glimpse of a large man with a weather-beaten face, wearing a peaked cap, as the carriage passed. This, I surmised, was Carpenter himself.

I got outside the docks with no further alarums, hailed a passing cab, and gave my destination as Scotland Yard. When I got there the luck which had been with me in the last hours ran out completely. Nobody that I saw had heard of Lestrade or Sherlock Holmes, and I was obliged to wait, fuming with impatience, while someone went upstairs to 'make enquiries'.

After what seemed a very long time, someone approached me and told me Lestrade was not in the building, but that if I cared to wait, a messenger would be despatched to fetch him.

I debated with myself for a few moments, as to whether I should tell my story to an officer who might not know the background of the case, and the special relationship which my friend had with Scotland Yard. However, this would inevitably take up a great deal of time, and I came to the conclusion that it would probably be quicker to await the arrival of Lestrade. I told the man I would wait, and seated myself, once again.

Another, seemingly lengthy, period of time passed, and I began to wish I had gone to the Admiralty instead, when, at last, Lestrade appeared. I outlined the situation, and managed to convey the sense of urgency which I felt.

Lestrade then proposed sending a wire to the nearest Coast-guard station to the Deptford quay, to the effect that they should send one of their fastest launches there to meet us. I was against the idea, but Lestrade insisted upon it.

After one of the fastest and most daring dashes through the crowded streets of London that I have ever experienced, we arrived at the quay, as breathless as the horses.

The ship had sailed.

I stood on the quay side, and the tears flowed down my cheeks, while sobs shook my frame to its core. The thought that I would never see my friend again was too much for me to bear. I sat on a bollard, my head in my hands, oblivious to all around me. After some minutes I came to myself a little, and I looked around me. A dozen or more constables, and two sergeants, who had been in carriages following more slowly behind us, stood a little way off, watching me with mixed expressions, having arrived while I was too preoccupied with worry to take any notice.

Several loud and piercing whistles from the direction of the water now distracted me, they arose from the steam-whistle of a Coast-guard cutter. I had silently cursed Lestrade, when he proposed delaying our departure from Scotland Yard in order to summon the cutter by wire, but now I had to restrain a powerful impulse to fall on his neck. Perhaps, after all, there was a chance that my friend could be saved.

Lestrade and I boarded the cutter, and immediately set off down the river, leaving the other men to await our return

We had reached the mouth of the Thames before we saw a three-masted ship which might prove to be the *Matilda*, but there were one or two others, and so it was impossible to tell.

Telescopes were brought to bear, and, below the taffrail of the most distant three-masted ship, the name *Matilda* could be discerned. We immediately set our course to coincide with hers.

The captain of the Coast-guard vessel, who had been appraised by Lestrade of the circumstances concerning the chase, remarked that it was just as well that those aboard the *Matilda* were unaware of our proximity and purpose, otherwise they would have obscured the name at the stern, in order to make pursuit more difficult, if not impossible.

Our quarry had established a considerable lead, and she was flying along under full sail with a fair wind. We were gaining on her, but the distance between us shortened very slowly. She appeared to be making for the coast of France.

After more than hour, when the distance between us was about a quarter of a mile, we clearly saw the flash of telescopes trained upon us, and a great bustle of activity on her deck. We had clearly taken her by surprise, but now lost that advantage. Soon afterwards, as we drew ever closer, we could see objects being thrown overboard. My heart was in my mouth, one of those objects could so easily be Holmes.

When we were within hailing distance of the *Matilda*, the captain shouted that she must heave to. When there was no response to this, we moved away until we were a hundred yards to one side, and slightly ahead. Then the small gun forward of the cutter was uncovered, and a shot was fired across her bows.

This brought the desired response, the sails were furled, and we circled around and came alongside.

Four of the cutter's crew scrambled up a boarding ladder dangling over the ship's side, Lestrade and I bringing up the rear. My foot was painful and the climb hurt me considerably.

When we assembled on deck we were met by the Captain, the large man with the weather-beaten face who had passed me in his carriage earlier that day, together with some of his crew. He was not pleased to see us.

"What is the meaning of this?" He thundered, with blazing eyes, and fists clenched at his sides.

"We have orders from Scotland Yard to detain this ship, and make a thorough search," said the Coast-guard captain.

"For what reason?"

"I am not obliged to divulge the reason, at this stage."

"Very well, you have my permission," said Carpenter, unexpectedly, adopting a less pugnacious tone and attitude. Perhaps the name of Scotland Yard had had a sobering effect.

"First, I want all hands on deck, and I want the ship's roster brought to me."

Carpenter nodded to a large, very ugly man, standing next to him. In a short while, all the men were standing in a ragged line, and the captain of the cutter stood with the roster book in his hands, and called out the name of each man listed, at the same time he demanded from Carpenter a brief description of the man's duties aboard. As each name was called, he was told to step forward, and when his duties had been given, he was dismissed to a place on deck near the wheel-house. Eventually, only one name, the last on the roster, remained, but there was no-one left in the line to claim it.

"Where is William Hanson?" demanded the cutter's captain.

My heart gave a leap. This was the false name adopted by my friend!

"He is below, sick, and is unable to attend this enquiry," said Carpenter.

"This man is a doctor," said the Coast-Guard captain, placing his hand on my shoulder. "He will attend Hanson. Please delegate someone to take him to the sick man's berth."

The ugly man was chosen as my guide, and I followed him below. I was hardly able to conceal my anticipation, despite the pain of my injury.

Holmes, for it proved to be he, was lying, unconscious, on a bed in a cabin, this cabin was not the one where he had been imprisoned. A brief examination told me that he had been drugged, probably with laudanum. His false papers were on a shelf above his bed.

I understood, at last, the stratagem of Carpenter. He was obviously going to try and bluff his way out of the difficult situation in which he now found himself. He had been able to throw overboard everything which connected him with the bank robbery, but obviously had not consigned the body of my friend to the deep. Perhaps he had been prevented from doing this, in the short time between the sighting of the Coast-guard vessel, and our coming alongside, by the very chains and padlocks with which Holmes had been so securely bound.

This was why there was no response, at first, to the order to heave to: Carpenter had needed a few minutes to think of a plan. He had added the name of William Hanson to the roster book, ordered Holmes drugged, and placed in this cabin. He would then deny all knowledge that the man was Holmes. He had papers to the effect that he was Hanson, after all, and it would be difficult to prove, even with my witness statement. I left the cabin, and went to confer with Lestrade and the captain of the cutter. The fact that objects had been thrown overboard as we approached in the cutter was not even mentioned. I assumed that the Coast-guard had seen similar things before, probably many times, and knew that it was not worth pursuing.

Our conference took place in the lee of a deck-house, while the other men from the cutter made a systematic search of the ship. They returned, after a long interval, empty-handed, as I thought they would.

I saw Carpenter approaching, he looked very pleased with himself. "Gentlemen, I must now ask you to leave this ship."

We looked at one another. The captain of the cutter showed signs of rage at this imperious request, and began to speak, but Carpenter held up his hand as if to silence him.

"If you would follow me, gentlemen," said Carpenter, "there is something which I desire you to see."

We followed him to the stern of the ship, where he pointed

to something in the water some distance off. Whatever it was, it was getting smaller and smaller as we left it behind.

The face of the Coast-guard captain assumed an expression of deep chagrin, and Lestrade and I looked at him in surprise.

"I can see from your expression, Captain, that I do not have to tell you what I shall now tell your companions. That buoy marks the end of British waters and the beginning of French. This ship has drifted some way into French jurisdiction, the water here being too deep for an anchor to hold, and you and your companions no longer have any authority on board. If you had formally arrested me while we were in British waters that would be a different story, but you did not, and I now ask you to leave."

"We must take William Hanson with us," I blurted out.

"Why would you want to do that?" asked Carpenter, with a malicious grin.

"He is ill, and needs medical attention ashore. That is my opinion as a doctor."

Carpenter considered for a few moments, his lips pursed. "And if I refuse?"

"Then I, for one, will stay on board until we put into a port, and see to it that he receives proper treatment." I was grasping at straws, but I could not think of anything else to say.

"Very well," said Carpenter, at last. "You have my permission to remove him."

As we carried Holmes, still insensible, to the cutter, it occurred to me that Carpenter had good reasons of his own for not wanting Holmes and myself on board when he put into his next port, no matter where that might be. He could, of course, have disposed of us both, in the manner he was going to dispose of Holmes. But perhaps he did not want to have a charge of murder on the high seas levelled at him, and a life-time of looking over his shoulder. Even as things stood, I did not see how he could ever return to the British Isles.

We made our way back to port. I felt utterly spent and washed out, and my companions felt much the same. As we steamed up the Thames Holmes awoke, but, when I reassured him that he was in safe hands, he drifted back into sleep.

Later that evening, Holmes, who had been asleep on our sofa, woke with a start, rubbed his eyes, and called for his pipe and tobacco, which I hastened to bring to him.

He sat up, filled and lit his pipe, and enquired how he came to be there. I gave him a brief account of the events which had occurred since I last saw him that day. He was still very groggy, but I managed to persuade him to have something to eat, and then retire for the night.

The next morning Holmes displayed a ravenous appetite and Mrs. Hudson was obliged to make several journeys up and down the stairs, to supply enough eggs and rashers of bacon to appease it. This she was glad to do, as she, like me, had been very concerned about him.

When his hunger abated, he seemed much like his usual self, and we sat on either side of the fire in order to hear his story. "As you know, I left here the evening before last to keep my appointment with Carpenter. I was armed with the knowledge I had crammed, regarding every aspect of diving, and also the false papers which gave me the identity of William Hanson.

"I was received by the captain, in a room which served him as a library and study. It had several nautical features, including Admiralty volumes concerned with navigation, rolls of charts, sextants, signal-flags, and a binnacle in the bay window. We seated ourselves on opposite sides of his desk. At first the conversation went quite well, he had my false papers on the desk before him, and he seemed to be quite taken in. I relaxed a little as we talked, and began, as covertly as I could, to scan the books in the shelves behind him. What should I see, amongst the books on a shelf dedicated to the natural sciences, but the very volume by Davy, which I had mentioned to you, that which dealt with the physiological and psychological effects of the inhalation of nitrous oxide. Next to it was a slim volume with lettering on the spine too small for me to read.

"At one point, Carpenter left the room for a few minutes, and I got up to look at the spine of the slim volume: it was Coxeter's catalogue. Once I had seen these two volumes, I was certain that I had found the man behind the robbery. It was as if these revelations broke the camel's back of my doubt, which in any case, by this time, was not very great. I cast around in my mind for some pretext, which would allow me to leave with this knowledge, so that I could formulate a plan to trap him.

"Hardly had I regained my seat, when the captain returned. The atmosphere of the room became decidedly chill. Perhaps I had been covertly observed, or it may be that Carpenter had somehow divined my new state of mind. He is, as I have said, an intelligent and shrewd man, with piercing, deep-set eyes, with heavy lids. It is of no real consequence, but I subsequently discovered that he is of Norwegian extraction, and I have found those features to be a strong characteristic of that race.

"He began to ask penetrating questions, in a way which would not have disgraced a barrister. These questions were to do with people and events of which I had no knowledge. Naturally, I found myself tongue-tied. Suddenly, to my intense chagrin, he stood up and pointed at me accusingly. 'You are Sherlock Holmes,' he said, in a stentorian voice.

"I stood up, also, but before I could gather my wits sufficiently to produce an argument which might convince him that he was wrong, three men burst in from an adjoining room, where they must have been listening to everything which occurred. They seized me, and tied my arms behind my back. Carpenter came out from behind his desk, and with a swift, decisive movement, removed my false beard. Once this was done, he scrutinised me with his face only about two feet from mine. I found this a little disconcerting. Then he drew back and nodded slowly, as if completely satisfied with his earlier announcement. I am still in the dark, as to how he knew me.

"He told me to be seated, once more. Two of the men took up positions at the doors, the other stood next to the binnacle and guarded the bay window. He asked me whether anyone knew that I had an appointment to see him that evening. I refused to answer, and he made a gesture of impatience. It was virtually a rhetorical question, because he now had to proceed as if some person or persons knew of my little adventure. He deliberated for a few moments, and then he told two of his men to take me below. As I was taken from the room, I saw him beckon to the third man, who then approached his desk. Just before the door was closed I heard Carpenter say: '... no sleep for any man to-night'.

"I was taken to a small, bare, cellar-room, fitted with a stout door. The door was locked, and I watched as the light from their lamp, which showed faintly around the edges of the door, grew fainter and fainter as they retraced their steps. I was then left in total darkness.

"I sat wrapped in the blankets, for it was very cold in the cellar. Hours passed, as best as I could judge, because I had no means of telling the time. Then, as I fell into a half-doze, I heard footsteps, and I was removed from the cellar by the same two men who had imprisoned me there. They gagged and blindfolded me at the head of the stairs which led to the cellar, and then they forced me to walk down some kind of paved path. I could feel the cold night air, and, even though I was blindfolded, I could tell that it was still dark.

"The men half-carried me on to some wooden structure, which felt, at first, like some kind of cart. Then, when I heard

92

lapping water, and felt a slight rocking motion, I knew that I was in a boat. I became aware of the smell of coal, oil, and hot metal, and soon afterwards the sound of an engine. The rushing noise of water at the sides of the boat told me that we were under way. After a long interval, I was hoisted, by means of a rope, up a wooden hull, and I knew that I was now on a ship. They carried me down a ladder and I was placed in a small cabin. My blindfold was removed, but my gag was not, and I was securely fastened to the wall by means of chains and padlocks. There was a great deal of activity on board, and, from snatches of conversation which I heard, I discovered that we were to embark that morning. The rest, of course, you know. But now it is your turn, you really must tell me how you came to find me."

I told him of the series of events which led me to the *Matilda*, and everything that had happened since then. He listened without comment.

"Well done, Watson," he said, when I had finished. "A very neat piece of work, I do not think I could have done better. I owe you my life." So saying, he leaned forward, and clasped my hand in a firm grip. I felt a lump rise in my throat.

After Holmes had released his hand, it was some time before I could trust myself to speak. "Where do you suppose Carpenter is bound?" I asked. I was not really interested in his fate. I only asked the question to mask the emotion which I still felt.

"Tortuga," replied Holmes, who seemed to divine my emotional state. "He has gone to investigate a sunken wreck near there."

Later that day, after Lestrade was appraised of the affairs of Carpenter, he went with some of his men to the house in Chelsea, but everything of value had gone. Further investigation revealed that the house had been mortgaged long before. Holmes had interfered somewhat with the plans of The Admiral, but had not managed to frustrate them. Lord Ephgrave was bitterly disappointed to hear the news of Carpenter, but he gave Holmes five hundred pounds, anyway, for expenses and inconveniences as he put it, when he heard of the tribulations which my friend had endured on his behalf.

More than five years have elapsed since I penned the above, and there has been no news of The Admiral, despite the most determined efforts to trace him. But, as Holmes remarked, a man of his calibre could very easily be living just down the road, for all that anyone knew. He is not convinced that he has seen the last of him.

The Adventure of the Quincunx Challenge

I strolled up Oxford Street on my way back to our rooms in Baker Street from Hyde Park. I had spent a leisurely hour or so there, sitting on a bench enjoying the late May sunshine.

Every so often, when I passed a news-vendor's stand, I saw that the same story, albeit in different words, formed the headlines of the day. The last I passed said: FOURTH WOMAN ABDUCTED. MYSTERY STILL UNSOLVED.

I removed my hat for a moment and wiped my brow, for it was a hot day. I entered 221B, made my way up the stairs to our apartment and went into the room which doubled as sitting- and consulting-room, when I saw that my friend, Sherlock Holmes, had received a visitor.

"I'm terribly sorry, Holmes," I said, turning to leave.

"My dear Watson," said Holmes. "Please come in. I am quite certain that this gentleman would have no objection to your presence."

Turning to his client, he said. "This is my colleague, Doctor Watson. You may say anything you have to say to me to him also. Watson, this is Mr. Alexander McClean."

"I have no objections whatsoever to the doctor's presence," said the visitor, a well-groomed young man, with a prosperous air about him. His top-hat, which stood on a nearby table, looked new and of good quality, as did the clothes he wore. However, his fresh face bore the marks of a profound sorrow, and redness about his eyes showed that he had been weeping within the last few hours. "Perhaps it would be best if I were to start from the beginning," he added.

And so when we were all seated comfortably, having removed our jackets because of the heat, and with the windows thrown open as wide as they would go, the young man began his narrative.

"Gentlemen," he began, "the young woman who has most recently disappeared, the person whose story forms the headlines in the press today is my dear sister, Elizabeth." Here he briefly closed his eyes, stifled a sob, swallowed hard, and resumed. "She went, alone, to a park concert yesterday afternoon, and never returned, I have been in contact since then with everyone who knows us, but none of them has seen her.

"I should mention that we live together in the house in Russell Square which our father left us when he died, our mother has been dead these five years. We are the only children of the marriage, and my sister keeps house for me, neither of us being married. She is a year younger than me, but is an eminently sensible girl, with a wise head on her shoulders.

"I am a junior partner in the firm of Aston and Hopkins, silk merchants, of Bond Street. My work frequently takes me out of town, and even abroad, but I have been in London all this week, and have been home every evening, and so I was in a position to notice her absence almost immediately."

Holmes and I murmured a few words of sympathy.

"Perhaps I should describe her," said our visitor, "she is..."

"She is small, dark, and very pretty," interposed Holmes.

"Why, yes, she is," said the young man in amazement. "But I don't see how you could possibly know that."

"There is no mystery about it," said Holmes, "all four women concerned in these abductions, who have disappeared in the past few weeks were young, pretty, small, and dark-haired. Also they all vanished during the hours of daylight from one central London park or another."

"Do you believe that all these kidnappings are the work of one man?" said I.

"I think it highly probable," said my friend.

"But what sort of man - it must be a man, I suppose - would have the bare-faced nerve to kidnap women from the parks of

London in broad daylight?" said our visitor, his outrage, for the moment, displacing his grief. "And for what reason?"

"That is what we must discover," said Holmes.

"But there are no clues," I exclaimed.

"For the time being, at least, we have no clues," said Holmes, nodding his head.

"I do not think we need to detain you any further," said Holmes to the young man. "I have your card, and the moment I know anything definite, I will be in touch."

Our visitor bowed to us both, and departed. He forgot his hat, and I was obliged to follow him downstairs in order to give it to him. I had already made a mental note of his abstracted state of mind, and I advised him, as a doctor, to seek out his own physician so that some kind of sedative could be prescribed, to help calm his nerves in the days ahead.

When I returned to our rooms, I found Holmes looking out of one of the open windows, with his hands in his pockets. I joined him there, and together we watched the young man, who had hailed a cab, getting into it.

Holmes shook his head. "This is a difficult type of case to solve," he said. "What appear to be totally random abductions."

That evening we had another visitor: Lestrade, who sat in a chair, fanning himself with his bowler, mopping his brow with a none too clean handkerchief. His interview with Holmes, which dealt with the abductions, afforded no new clues and after a short time he left.

The next morning Holmes was up betimes, scanning the papers for anything which pertained to the disappearances. One journalist had been contacted by a young lady who answered the general description of the other missing women. She told of a meeting at the park concert in question, with a large, middle-aged man with an educated accent, dressed like a gentleman. This man had tried to persuade her to accept a ride home in his carriage after the concert was over. She had refused, despite the fact that the man had been accompanied by a dark-haired young woman, whom the man had introduced as his daughter. The reporter concluded that she had had a lucky escape.

"This then is our only clue," said Holmes, as we discussed the story at breakfast.

The mid-morning post brought a curious letter, which purported to be written by the abductor of the women. It was post-marked 11 the previous evening in north London. The address was written in a neat, precise hand, in green ink, and referred to my friend as: 'Clever Mr. Sherlock Holmes'. The typewritten letter, if genuine, seemed to pose a challenge of some kind.

> I have heard of you, Holmes, you busybody. (it read)
> Always poking your long nose into everyone's affairs.
> I live in Sutton, does that help you?
> Let us see if you can catch me, before it is quincunx.
> The fan belongs to my latest acquisition.
> Be at Radlett station at ten to-night.
> On the down platform.

It was unsigned, but in the lower right-hand corner, just below the text, was a small blob of gold-coloured sealing-wax bearing the imprint of a strange symbol, a circle with a sceptre that appeared to be a stylised lightning-bolt, while the head was a flaming orb. The letter and matching envelope were light blue. It also contained an enclosure: a fragment of an ivory fan.

"We are dealing with a madman, Holmes!" I exclaimed, having read the letter. "And what does he mean by quincunx?"

"Quincunx," said Holmes, "is a design or arrangement of five items, so that four are at the corners of a square, the fifth in the centre. Clearly he challenges me to catch him before he makes five his total. Sutton, by the way, is the most common name of towns in this country, and is unlikely to get us very far, even if he really does live in a place of that name."

Holmes took the letter and envelope over to the window to examine them carefully in the better light there, with the aid of a convex lens. While he stood there, there was a flash of light from outside, followed almost immediately by a rumble of thunder. The hot, dry spell was obviously drawing to a close.

"Do you propose to keep the appointment?"

"I will call upon Mr. McClean to-day, and ask him if he recognises this fragment of fan," he replied, over his shoulder, "and if he does, I shall, most assuredly, keep the appointment. I would be glad, in that case, if you would accompany me to Radlett, and bring your service revolver with you.

"There is very little to be gleaned from the letter and envelope, save that they are both of good quality paper. But we shall keep them both safe, in the event that we find the typewriter, pen and ink-bottle which were used."

Holmes put the letter to his nose, and sniffed deeply. "There is no scent or smell of any kind," he remarked, as he put the letter, envelope and enclosure in a new envelope, and then placed it in the pocket of his jacket, which was hanging up.

Holmes then finished dressing and, pausing only to select a large umbrella from our meagre stock, went out. Outside, the first large raindrops were falling.

It was after mid-day when Holmes returned, damp and bedraggled. He placed the dripping umbrella in the stand, and went into his bedroom to change. When he emerged, towelling his hair vigorously, he was clad in a dressing gown and slippers. He flopped into a chair and threw the towel into a corner.

"It *is* a piece of Miss McClean's fan," said he without preamble. "Her brother gave her a matching pair of such fans last Christmas."

"Does this mean that we will go to Radlett tonight?" I asked.

"It does."

Holmes got up from his chair to get a pipe, vestas, and tobacco. I sat opposite him, while he filled his pipe and lit it.

"Do you think that we are dealing with a madman?" I asked, breaking the silence.

Holmes took the pipe from his lips, and considered for a few moments before speaking. "It is my opinion that we are certainly dealing with a man suffering from monomania, or an *idée fixe*," said he. "Also he is arrogant, with a very high opinion of himself and his abilities. He has no doubts whatsoever that he can defeat me - let alone the official police - he would not write letters to me of that kind if he did not. He knows of my reputation, that is clear from the ironic form of address: 'Clever Mr. Sherlock Holmes'. Last but not least, there is the matter of the sealing-wax impression, which an acquaintance of mine was kind enough to identify this morning. It is an emblem of sovereignty of both Greek and Roman gods, as well as the symbol of a god who is the father of a family. *Ergo*, he believes he is a god of sorts. A person elevated high above the common herd. We know he is a father because he introduced his daughter to a potential victim. The sealing-wax was gold, which further underlines his attitude towards the rest of humanity. And yet, for all his arrogance and conceit, he feels a sense of inferiority. It shows itself in his challenge to me. A truly clever man would not need to do that."

"That is wonderful, Holmes," I exclaimed.

Holmes sighed, he appeared to be bored. "Oh," he said, "I forgot to mention that I showed the letter, envelope and enclosure to Lestrade. He will accompany us to-night, but will keep out of the way. He is going to the station with two plain-clothes men. He will travel there independently of us, and, as far as possible, will conceal himself and his men. I only hope he makes a good job of it, we do not want to frighten off our kidnapper, or whatever he is."

As soon as we stepped outside our door that evening at eight Holmes engaged a cab as our means of transport there and back. The rain had stopped, and we rattled through wet, glistening streets. There was now that high humidity which comes when a shower has fallen after a few hot days, and I soon felt rather damp and sticky. Holmes, however, seemed to be unaffected.

We had the long journey of about fifteen miles to Radlett ahead of us, but when I had asked Holmes why we could not go by train he simply said that that was what our adversary would expect us to do, and refused to discuss it further.

At a quarter to the appointed hour, we stood on the down platform of Radlett station, empty save for a man sweeping out the waiting room. Holmes, on arrival, had spent some time examining the station time-tables, and remarked that no train was scheduled to stop there, on any platform, at ten o'clock.

There was no sign of Lestrade or his men, and it looked as it my companion's hopes had been fulfilled in that direction at least. We seated ourselves at last, some way down the platform, just inside the range of the gas lamps, so that we could be seen, but also so that we could quickly conceal ourselves if necessary.

Time passed, ten o'clock came and went, Holmes and I no longer conversed, and I started to feel uneasy - was this just a wild goose chase?

Then, just after five minutes past the hour, I was aware of a faint sound a long way off in the stillness of the night: it was the sound of a fast-approaching train. It thundered into the station, blowing its whistle as it did so. Judging by its speed it was an express, and as it rushed past us, we could see that there were very few passengers. The lights in the carriages flickered on our faces, and the breeze caused by its movement made me reach for my hat. As the last carriage flashed past, I saw a large man standing, hatless, at an open window. Just before the point where the train would be hidden by the darkness, an arm reached out and threw something in our direction, something which skidded and rolled on the platform, coming to rest about ten yards from us.

Holmes approached the small parcel, for so it turned out to be, with great caution and, as he did, Lestrade and his men emerged from the shadows at the end of the platform.

Holmes and Lestrade stood looking at the parcel together from a few feet away. Both seemed reluctant to handle it. Finally Holmes stooped and picked it up.

"Had it contained anything which might harm us, it would probably have shown signs of it after the impact of its fall," he announced, to no-one in particular.

We all trooped into the now deserted waiting room. Holmes placed the parcel on a table, and turned it over a number of times to thoroughly examine it. It was wrapped in brown paper, and tied up with string. The wrapping had been damaged in the fall on to the platform, revealing the corner of a box of polished, dark wood. The string was sealed with the same gold sealing wax that we had seen before. Written on the wrapping, in green ink, were the letters S. H..

Holmes cut the string with a pocket knife in order to preserve the knot, and removed the brown paper, which action revealed a finely carved, wooden box, which appeared to be of Indian manufacture, with a brass catch and hinges. Very slowly, he unfastened the catch and raised the lid. Inside was something wrapped in tissue paper, which Holmes slowly unwrapped. Inside it was a playing card: the five of spades. Written on it in green ink was a question mark. There was nothing else in the box.

We rattled back to Baker Street in the hired cab. Holmes was taciturn, almost sullen. He sat, smoking his pipe, and every now and then a street lamp briefly illumined his aquiline features, which were creased into a frown.

He had retained the box, card and the various wrappings from the parcel, and had announced his intention of subjecting them to further scrutiny.

When we got back to Baker Street, Holmes took a large sheet of white paper, and placed it on our dining table. He then placed upon it the various parts which had made up the parcel, and examined them each in turn with a convex lens by the light of our best lamp. When he was in the process of examining the box, he gave an exclamation.

"Have you found anything?" I asked.

"One part of the underside of this box, near one corner, has been carefully filed away," he replied.

"To remove the maker's mark?" I suggested.

"I believe that was the intention, Watson. The filing has been done to such a depth that the name cannot have been simply written, or stamped with a rubber stamp, it must have been done with a metal punch, or punches." He paused, as if to consider. "There is just a chance..."

Holmes jumped up, and went to the chemical corner, where he found a retort, poured into it some water from a carafe, and set it over a spirit lamp. While he waited for the water to boil, he explained to me that if the maker's name had been stamped into the box, the grain of the wood would bear the imprint of the stamp for some considerable depth, and that although it had been obliterated by the file, the use of steam would raise the grain and reveal what had been impressed there.

The water in the retort soon boiled, and Holmes held the filed corner to the orifice at the end of the neck of the retort from which a jet of steam now issued forth. After a little while, the grain of the wood began to rise, and we could just make out the name, 'J. Devi'.

Holmes took down a commercial directory from our shelves, and found an entry: Devi, Jaswant, and Sons, Importers of Genuine Indian Goods, 273 Bethnal Green Road, Shoreditch.

Holmes put the cap back on the lamp, and sat down in an armchair. Something grim and determined about his manner told me that he now regarded this case as a straight fight between two individuals, just as surely as if they were two bare-knuckled pugilists facing each other across the ring.

"I shall call upon the firm of Jaswant Devi and Sons first thing tomorrow morning," he announced at length. "But it is past one, and now, I think, we could do with a good night's sleep."

The next morning was fine and bright, and it seemed that the storm of the previous day had only been a temporary respite from the ever-increasing heat of the days which had preceded it. We breakfasted at eight and then Holmes went out. I sat on at the table after breakfast, reading the papers in the bright sunshine which streamed through our windows. There was nothing in any of them about the abductions.

It was early evening before Holmes returned, he seemed tired and out of sorts. He changed into his dressing gown, and sat in the armchair with his pipe.

"Any luck, Holmes?" I enquired.

"I have been all over London today," he answered, and he seemed to be talking to himself alone, "particularly north London, where I feel sure our true researches lie. Consider the post-mark of that curious letter, and the fact that Radlett lies to the north. It is possible that he is laying a false scent. However, he patently wants to give us some information, however small the amount may be. It is in his nature to make us follow him, the trick is to make sure that we do not get too close, and so I think he probably does live somewhere in the north of London."

"But the box Holmes, did it not furnish us with a clue?"

"I will give you an account of where the box led me," said he, "but first I must have something to eat." Accordingly he rang the bell and, when Mrs. Hudson came in answer to this summons, asked for cold ham, pickles, and a glass of beer.

I waited patiently while he consumed this, and then we settled ourselves in chairs on opposite sides of the empty fireplace.

"I went to the firm of Jaswant Devi and Sons," he began, "who were very helpful. They are wholesalers, but were able to provide me with a list of people to whom they supplied the boxes. It was one of a consignment of one hundred, which they received from India just over two years ago - they have had none quite like it, before or since. The design on the lid, that of a figure dancing inside a fiery circle, represents the god Shiva. So far so good. It is possible, by the way, that because the design on the box represents a god, it fits into the theory that the abductor thinks himself to be above the common herd.

"The firm had supplied these boxes to some thirteen retail outlets, six in the northern part of the capital. Today I visited all thirteen, but naturally paid more attention to those six. At each I asked if they could recall selling those boxes, to a large, middle-aged gentleman, with an educated accent. Unfortunately nobody could recollect doing so, and I drew a complete blank."

Holmes paused at this point, rubbing his eyes, he did seem to be more than a little weary. I offered him my cigarette case, and when he had lit up, and smoked one for a minute or so, he seemed to rally a little.

"It is perhaps significant," he went on, "that one of the shops was within a mile of Radlett station, and I mean to go there again before very long, to see if I can jog anyone's memory."

I reflected again that the unusual energy shown by my friend in this case was because his blood was up, and I began to have misgivings as to whether his constitution could stand the strain.

Later, Holmes once again got out the sheet of paper, placed the components of the parcel on it, and subjected them to the most exacting scrutiny, using a variety of lenses. I watched him anxiously.

Finally he sat back in his chair with a long sigh, rubbing his eyes. He then got up, and with a peremptory salutation of 'good night', which I only just had time to return, withdrew to his bedroom.

The next morning dawned bright and clear, and despite the early hour at which Holmes and I breakfasted, the heat was already quite oppressive. Just after we had finished our breakfast, the second post arrived. Among the letters was one in violet ink. Again it was addressed to 'Clever Mr. Sherlock Holmes', again it was typewritten, and this time the letter and envelope were of white paper.

> I saw you at the station. (it read)
> Do you know what day it is to-day?
> It is the quincunx of May.

There was no enclosure this time. The gold sealing-wax blob with the symbol was in the bottom right-hand corner, just under the text as before. Holmes became grey with anger as we read it together.

"We both know what this means," he said. "He intends to find another unfortunate victim to-day. I will tell Lestrade to have extra men on patrol. He had arranged to have posters and handbills printed, warning young ladies to be on their guard against strange men offering rides in their carriages, but there has not been sufficient time to have them distributed. It is just too frustrating for words." So saying, he went out.

I waited for Holmes's return throughout that hot, interminable day. But before he returned, I read in the late editions of the evening papers that, despite the warning Holmes had received, another young woman had been abducted, this time from St. James's Park. The headlines seemed to scream: FIFTH WOMAN MISSING, and some had the subheading: CHALLENGE TO SHERLOCK HOLMES. It had become a *cause celèbre*. My friend finally came back at about ten o'clock. He was utterly exhausted, drawn, and dispirited. My fears for his health redoubled, and despite his protests, I rang down for some food, and made sure he drank some brandy after it.

After he had had this refreshment, he told me a little of what had been done, in vain, to prevent another kidnapping. "Lestrade and I worked hand-in-glove to-day," said he. "He had over one hundred extra men in the parks alone, since all the abductions have taken place from parks. He and I personally travelled from park to park all day, until that is, we were informed that despite our best efforts, another victim had been taken." There was more than a touch of bitterness in his voice as he pronounced this last, a bitterness which was tempered with extreme weariness.

Later, when he was more himself, he compared the typewritten note which had arrived that morning with the previous message. In so doing he made the discovery that they were written on two different typewriting machines.

"See, Watson," he cried, beckoning me to the table where he was working, and handing me one of his lenses, "there are no less than eight differences in these two examples. The tail of the q in the word quincunx, for instance, is missing almost entirely in this second communication. The dot under the question mark is also absent. I will not bore you with the other differences, but it is clear that two machines have been used. Since the similarities far outweigh the differences, I think it is safe to assume that the two machines are of the same make, one, perhaps, older than the other, with worn letters."

"Does it help in any way?" I asked.

"I am forced to admit that it does not get us much further, the number of typewriters now in London must run into the hundreds, if not the thousands. However, it is still an important clue. When we catch this man we will be able to compare these typescripts with those produced by any machines he may have had access to."

Holmes fell silent, obviously deep in thought. I could not help but discern a note of optimism in his use of the word 'when' rather than 'if' in the last sentence.

"What kind of man has two typewriters or access to two machines?" he mused, abruptly coming out of his reverie. "I think that there is something which I have overlooked."

"A businessman, perhaps?" I hazarded, "with access to an office or offices."

"Possibly," said my friend slowly, and relapsed into deep thought again.

The conversation languished after that, and Holmes and I retired for the night. The next thing that I remember, after falling asleep, was a hand shaking my shoulder. I sat up with a start. It was Holmes, carrying a candlestick. I could see by my watch that it was half past three in the morning.

"What the deuce is the matter, Holmes?" I exclaimed indistinctly, my brain still clouded by sleep.

"I have been a dolt, that is what is the matter," said he.

"What on earth do you mean?" I asked grumpily. I was in no mood for a discussion at this hour.

"Our kidnapper is a stationer," said Holmes. "Or at any rate he deals with stationery or office equipment in some way. That is what has been hidden in those notes of his, using different coloured inks, different typewriters, different stationery. There may even be a play on words in his demand that we go to Radlett *station*."

As soon as he had conveyed this information to me, he left my room, closing the door behind him. Many minutes passed before I fell asleep once more.

The next morning there was no sign of Holmes: he had evidently gone out at a very early hour, and I found that I was left to my own devices once more. I spent some time reading the story of the previous day's crime in the papers. The accounts were more rounded and fuller than those I had read the day before, which, owing to the small amount of time available, had been somewhat sketchy.

Towards two, Holmes returned with a bundle of books and papers under his arm. He made no reference to our encounter in the small hours, and I felt no inclination to mention it.

"This," said he, "is a complete list of London stationers, suppliers of office equipment, and the like. Anyone who is, or has been, in this line of business at any time from ten years ago to the present day is here. Somewhere in these lists, I feel certain, is the name of our kidnapper."

It was a considerable mass of paper.

Holmes set to work at our dining table, he began by selecting from the lists all those businesses which were, or had been, in north London. After about four hours, the list was complete. He would probably have taken less time, had not several representatives from the press arrived at our door desirous for some kind of statement from him about the challenge posed by the kidnapper. He was obliged to grant each an interview, to his great vexation and chagrin.

The final total of north London businesses, past and present, came to seventy-eight.

"I will begin with these," he said, "and if I draw a blank, I will turn my attention to those remaining."

Working on the assumption that our man was an independent retailer or wholesaler, he eliminated, for the time being, all those in the list who were old-established, household names with multiple outlets. This reduced the total to fifty-six.

By the time all this was done, it was past eight o'clock, and much too late to begin the task of canvassing the various firms about the kidnapper.

Holmes spent the rest of the evening, before retiring for the night, in an ill-concealed mood of anticipation and frustration, like a racehorse champing at the bit before the off. Mindful of his uncertain mental state, and worried about his well-being, I tried to converse with him about subjects which were not to do with the case in order to take his mind off it. In this I had limited success.

The next morning Holmes was obliged to remain in our rooms until nine, to await the arrival of Lestrade, with whom he was to discuss a systematic operation, which would result in all the stationers and related businesses being visited in one day. Holmes himself was to visit twelve of the firms, while Lestrade and several plain-clothes men would take care of the rest.

Holmes paced up and down in front of our fireplace, with growing impatience, he had hardly slept the night before, and refused to eat anything for breakfast.

At a quarter to the hour of Lestrade's arrival, a further communication from the abductor was brought up by Mrs. Hudson. It was easily recognisable, being addressed to 'Clever Mr. Sherlock Holmes', the address was written in red ink on a pale green envelope. Holmes tore it open, and we read it together.

> Now I hAve seven. (it read)
> My faMily is ComplEte.
> This is the lAst you will heAr of Me.
> We shall disapPear inTo the outer darkness.

110

The seal was there in gold sealing wax, in the same position as before.

"What does this mean," I exclaimed, "and why does he speak of seven, when only five have been abducted?"

Holmes took the typewritten letter to the window, where the bright sunshine streamed in. He was still standing there when Lestrade was shown up, He turned from the window at this interruption, with his brows furrowed, and his mind, if I was any judge of his demeanour, racing. Silently he handed the letter to Lestrade.

"What's this," said he, after glancing at it, "more gibberish from your friend and mine?"

"I am sorry, Lestrade," said my friend, "but I must ask you to postpone the visits to the stationers until I have discovered what this last message means. I believe that, if I can unravel it, a great deal of time and manpower can be saved."

Lestrade looked very put out by this, but he was used to my friend's peculiarities, and grudgingly nodded his assent.

Holmes got out the other typewritten messages and settled down at the dining table to compare them and also, presumably, to wrest some meaning from the last of them. It was as if, for him, we had ceased to exist.

Lestrade and I watched him for a while, and then Lestrade took his departure, promising to call in that evening for any further news.

Holmes fetched a sheet of paper and wrote something on it, referring to that morning's communication as he did so. He then sat for some time gazing at what he had written.

"This last note has been written on a typewriter which has a totally different typeface from the other two," remarked my friend at length. He rose to his feet, and selected a pipe from the rack. When he had filled it and got it going well, he sat in an armchair and placed the last communication from the madman, as I had begun to think of him, on his lap, together with the sheet of paper he had written on.

"What do you make of this, Watson?" he asked, handing me the sheet of paper.

I took it from him, and saw that he had written the letters: A, A, A, C, E, M, M, P, T.

"Those letters are present in the note in the form of capital letters, where one would not expect to find capitals," said he. "I have written them in alphabetical order."

"Are they an anagram perhaps?" I enquired.

"I do not think so," said Holmes. "I have tried to see if a word, or words, can be formed from them, but nothing springs to mind."

"I must beg you not to disturb me for an hour," he went on, "This is, at the very least, a two-pipe problem."

Holmes leaned back in his chair with his eyes closed, his face expressionless. There was nothing to show that he was awake, except the rhythmic puffing of his pipe. When at length the tobacco was exhausted he rose to refill it, returning at once to his meditative state in the armchair. I remained silent the whole of this time. The only activity I allowed myself, was to see if I could arrange the letters on the paper into a meaningful message, I could not, and I placed it quietly on a table.

Holmes's second pipe been cold for some considerable time before he showed any signs of life. He placed the pipe on a table, and in a languid fashion, rubbed his eyes and stretched.

"Have you formed any opinion as to the meaning of those letters?" I asked.

"Oh, that," said he, in a way that suggested that he had long since solved that problem and allowed his thoughts to dwell on other things, "there is no difficulty about that. It is an astronomical reference." Holmes was obviously in one of those moods of his in which a conversation was an uphill struggle.

"An astronomical reference to what, exactly?" I persisted.

"If you will kindly hand me the volume of the encyclopædia pertaining to P, I would be grateful," said he by way of reply.

I did as he asked, and after turning the pages, he handed me the book, indicating the relevant entry with his thumb. While he sat with his eyes closed, his fingertips together, I sat opposite and read the entry in question. It was headed: PLEIADES and said in part: "...a star cluster, supposed to represent Atlas and Pleione, with their seven daughters, Alcyone, Asterope, Celaeno, Electra, Maia, Merope, and Taygeta."

"This then, explains the initial letters," said I.

Holmes nodded, his eyes remained closed. He seemed calmer and more relaxed than at any time since the investigation began. "This latest piece of information has cost our correspondent the secret of his identity," said my friend, his eyes open once more.

"You know who he is?" I exclaimed incredulously.

"He has been arrogant," said Holmes, "and his arrogance has made him careless. He could not possibly have known that I had formed the opinion that he was connected with the stationery trade in some way, and this supposition, together with that last note, enabled me to unmask him."

Holmes rose to his feet, and showed me the list of stationers and related businesses, which he had compiled the previous evening. Among them was the name: Atlas Office Equipment and Stationery Ltd. Proprietor: Arthur T. Lassinger, 560 Station Road, Edgware, Middlesex.

"When I studied this list yesterday evening, I made a mental note to pay particular attention to the Atlas company, in fact I was going to make it my first port of call to-day. It is named after a god, something which aroused my attention, especially when I took into account the character of the man we were seeking. I have already spoken of the fact that he considers himself to be of god-like status. The note of this morning, referred to a family, and also to the outer darkness. I realised that this last was a reference to the heavens, and, in all probability, to a constellation. The only constellation in the heavens which pertains to a family, a family moreover with seven daughters, is the Pleiades, the paterfamilias of which was Atlas. You will also observe, Watson, that the first two initials, together with the three letters of his surname, spell out the word Atlas. We see here the seeds of a derangement which must have been sown in his childhood."

I realised now, why such a calmness had descended on my friend, and I was not at all surprised when Holmes announced that we were leaving immediately for Edgware.

As we travelled north, I asked Holmes again why the last note had referred to the correspondent now having seven, young women presumably, when in fact only five had been abducted. It was his opinion that the man had two natural daughters, and that he had wished, for some inexplicable reason, to make the number up to seven. He referred to the lucky escape of the young woman at the park concert where the fourth young woman was abducted. The report had said that the large man was accompanied by a young woman, whom he had introduced as his daughter. Holmes asserted that she probably really was his daughter, because it was not conceivable that she was one of the first three victims. This being the case, then the madness, or whatever it was, must have affected the whole family. He believed, that before the business was over, we would find that he had two natural daughters.

We alighted at Edgware, and quickly found the address referred to in the list he had prepared, this proved to be a greengrocery business. Enquiries established that there had been an office requisites and stationery business at that address, but that it had ceased trading some six months ago. No one knew of the exact whereabouts of Lassinger, but one man who had known him slightly - it appeared that he had been rather a self-effacing man with few friends - told us that the stationer lived in a large detached house outside St. Albans.

Holmes and I were hot on the trail now, and we went back to Edgware station to catch a train to St. Albans, which short journey took us through Radlett station.

When we arrived at St. Albans we went to the main post office, where we were able to find Lassinger's exact address. It appeared that he lived in a large villa, Mercator House, standing in its own walled grounds, about a mile from the town centre. Thither we directed our steps. When we had walked what seemed to be a considerable distance down a leafy lane, we came to the corner of an old stone wall, which followed the lane in one direction, while it also ran at right angles to it, across some fields. This wall, about eight feet high, was in a state of some disrepair, the top foot or so having crumbled away. This decay had been aided by the growth of shrubs and small trees.

At length we came to a point in the wall where there were two heavy, cast-iron gates, which were corroded by rust. A cracked and weathered, wooden signboard affixed to the wall, to the right of the gates, bore the name: Mercator House.

Holmes and I peered through the bars of the gates. Just inside them, and to the right, was the almost totally ruined gate house, its roof timbers exposed, like the ribs of some leviathan. In the middle distance, we could just make out the chimneys of the house, which was set in a wooded dell, a little below the level of the lane. There were no signs of life.

"It seems that the fortunes of the Lassinger family have been in a state of decline for many years," remarked Holmes.

"What do you propose to do now, Holmes?" I asked.

"We must go back to St. Albans, without any delay," replied my friend. "We have already taken a considerable risk in coming to the house, not so much a risk to ourselves, although even that was considerable, but rather, to the unfortunate young women who are almost certainly held captive there."

"I don't quite see what you mean," said I, surprised.

"We are dealing with a species of lunatic, of that there is no doubt," said Holmes, who had started to walk at a brisk pace back down the lane to the town, looking over his shoulder to make sure that I was following him. "But whatever else he may be, he is not stupid. Remember, he saw us at Radlett station, and he would probably recognise us if he saw us in this lane, and in so doing, be driven to some desperate act to cover his tracks for all time."

I reflected, for a while, on the unpleasant consequences for everyone concerned, in the event that we should be seen and recognised in the lane, and these thoughts caused me to become quite agitated. So much so, that when I heard horses approaching, I practically dragged Holmes into some bushes, until they had passed. They turned out to be those of a local brewery, pulling a dray.

I, for one, was profoundly glad when we had left the lane, and reached a more populated thoroughfare. When we reached the town, Holmes and I took refreshment in a little tea-shop, wherein Holmes outlined his plans.

He wanted me to return to Baker Street by the next available train. He was going to remain in St. Albans until nightfall, and then he would go back to Mercator House, climb over the wall, and do a little judicious spying. I, of course, wanted to go with him, but he would not hear of it.

"Consider this, Watson," he said, "if we both went there to-night, and came to grief at the hands of Lassinger, there would be no-one to raise the alarm and tell of what we have discovered. No, I must go alone. There is a train back to London at one in the morning and I fully intend to be on it.

"There is just one more thing," he went on, "Lestrade announced his intention of calling in this evening for further developments. I would be very much obliged if you do not breathe a word to him about our expedition to-day. I shall acquaint him with the facts of this matter on the morrow."

And so we parted at the door of the tea-shop. I watched him walk away without a backward glance. He had never seemed more vulnerable and alone.

I reached Baker Street about seven. The evening was fine and clear, but its beauty was lost to me, I thought only of my friend and the possible dangers he might face. At some time in that evening of deep anxiety, Lestrade called. I managed to deflect his inevitable questions about my friend, not, however, with as much skill as I would have liked, the result being that he left our rooms in a surly and suspicious state of mind.

The hours dragged by, two o'clock passed, and then three. Despite everything, I must have fallen into a fitful sleep in an armchair, because the next thing I remembered was the sound of a familiar voice.

I was overjoyed to see Holmes safe and sound, and would fain have embraced him. His mood was jubilant, and I knew that all had gone well for him that night. His right hand was roughly bandaged with a handkerchief, through which blood had seeped, and one of his trouser legs was torn at the knee. When I asked him about these injuries, he dismissed them as trifles.

"Are those girls being held at Mercator House?" I enquired, as soon as I was able to collect my thoughts after my slumber.

"They are," said he, sitting heavily down into a chair.

I hesitated before I asked the next question. "Are they safe and well?"

"For the moment they are, but there is no time to waste. I learned enough to know that we must act as soon as possible, preferably to-night."

117

Holmes was unwilling to discuss the subject further, and soon withdrew to his bedroom for a few hours sleep, after advising me to do the same.

When I awoke later that same morning, Holmes had already left, leaving me a note to the effect that he had gone to Scotland Yard, to liaise with Lestrade about the best way to approach the situation in St. Albans.

Holmes returned before noon with the plans finalised. He had become increasingly etiolated in the previous twenty four hours, and I was glad that the events of the night to come, would, in one way or another, bring an end to this curious affair.

And so it was, that shortly after nightfall, Holmes and I, accompanied by Lestrade, a local police inspector, and some twenty constables, found ourselves in a little wood, adjacent to the rear of the walled grounds of the Lassinger house. I found myself possessed by an almost unbearable tension, coupled inextricably with anticipation, whether originating within me, or communicated by the combined feelings of our group, I could not tell.

Shortly after ten, Holmes, Lestrade and I, together with a dozen of the constables, climbed over the back wall of the grounds, using two ladders which were then removed to a distant point in the wood. The other constables from the local force, under the command of their Inspector, took up strategic positions outside the wall. Holmes's foreboding had been fully taken into account, and nothing had been left to chance.

Once inside the grounds, Lestrade's constables divided into two groups of six. One group was to position themselves at one of the two rear entrances to the house, the other at the front entrance. Each group had sledgehammers with which to break in. Holmes, Lestrade and I were to be admitted to the house through the third and last entrance by a constable, as soon as the two groups were inside. They were to go in simultaneously on a prearranged signal from Lestrade.

Once we were all in our respective positions, Lestrade gave the signal: a prolonged note from a police whistle. At once there was the sound of sledgehammers on wood, accompanied by shouts of encouragement from the men breaking down the doors. Holmes had ascertained, during his foray the previous evening, that no dogs were kept at the house. The noise, in the stillness of that place, was tremendous and I caught the sound of the horses in the nearby stables neighing with fright.

The house had been in complete darkness, but I saw a light spring up in one of the first floor bedrooms, quickly followed by a second, much more intense light on the ground floor, which brightly illuminated the doorway at the end of the long passage beyond the barred windows to the right of our door, to which the door clearly gave access.

The hammering died down and then ceased. Soon afterwards two dark figures, silhouetted against the flickering yellow-orange light, appeared in the doorway at the top of the passage and made their way towards our door. I heard the sound of bolts being drawn and the door suddenly opened, revealing two of the uniformed men. They turned and led the way back into the house, we three following.

When we reached the principal stairwell of the house, which was thick with smoke, we saw that the bright light which had flared up on the ground floor was due to the fact that the staircase was a mass of roaring flames, so that it was impossible to ascend by them. There was a distinct smell of petroleum-ether in the air, which partly explained why the fire had taken such a powerful hold in such a short time.

Holmes immediately took charge and, after a pump had been found in the scullery, organised a chain with all the available men. We used anything that would hold water as buckets and several times Holmes risked injury when he advanced almost to the seat of the blaze with wet cloths wrapped around his head and legs to throw water over the unburnt upper part of the stairs to prevent the fire spreading on to the landing above.

While these activities were at their height, we all heard a hideously loud explosion from a room a few yards from the foot of the stairs. The door proved to be locked and, having no time to investigate further, we continued to fight the fire. At length we extinguished the last of the flames and left the smoke-filled stairwell to sit on the steps outside the shattered front doors. What a sight we made in the light of a few lamps! Everywhere were blackened faces and hands, singed clothes and hair.

We had been there for only a few moments when Holmes bethought himself of the explosion we had heard. Again, two constables and their sledgehammers were brought into play. When the broken door swung back on its hinges we found ourselves staring wordlessly at the crumpled figure of a large, thick-set man lying on a Indian rug, near a heavy mahogany desk, upon which two lamps burned. Clutched in the hand of the dead man, who was horribly wounded in the head, was a flintlock duelling pistol. On the desk, which had a tooled and gilded leather panel in its top, stood a box containing the other pistol, with the usual accoutrements. Also on the desk were two typewriting machines, while a third stood on a side table.

When he had recovered himself sufficiently, Lestrade sent the men back to join the others with the object of finding the whereabouts of the young women and anyone else who might be in the building.

The room in which the man lay was opulently furnished and appointed, its grandeur, however, was somewhat faded, and dust lay on several of its surfaces. A handsome library of leather-bound books, on shelves around three of the walls, was darkened by years of tobacco smoke and cobwebs festooned the high ceiling. Holmes threw open the window to allow the powder smoke to disperse.

Lestrade, after perfunctorily glancing round the study, went off to join his men, leaving Holmes and I alone.

A few minutes later, shouts of 'Holmes!' brought us out of the study, whereupon, looking up, we saw Lestrade, somewhat obscured by lingering smoke, on the first-floor landing. He announced that they had found a middle-aged woman, probably Lassinger's wife, and two young women in a bedroom. They were dead: poisoned with cyanide.

We ran upstairs to join Lestrade, who led us into one of the bedrooms, where we found the women lying side-by-side on a large, four-poster bed, Holmes picked up a large, one-pound jar labelled 'potassium cyanide 95%', which had been standing on a dressing-table, next to a carafe of water, its stopper beside it. He sniffed at it and replaced the stopper. On the floor lay a tumbler, which bore traces of liquid and white crystals, I picked it up and found it gave off the familiar odour of bitter almonds. Clearly this glass had been shared by the unfortunate women. In the bedside cabinet, we found a similar jar of the poison.

I fervently hoped that the two young women were not among the number of those who had been abducted, and that they would prove to be Lassinger's two natural daughters. It was not that I was unmoved by their demise - I was, but the tragedy would have been greater in the former case.

At this point a constable ran into the room in a very excited state to say that they had found the young women imprisoned in two adjoining rooms and that they had been released.

We followed the constable to the rooms, and came upon a scene that I will never forget. The joy of the poor girls, when they realised that they were safe, was extremely moving. Again and again they expressed their tearful gratitude to the rescuers in general and my friend in particular on being told of his part in the affair. Holmes had some difficulty in coping with their effusive praise, but in the event, he acquitted himself quite well.

Arrangements were soon made to convey the women to a police station in the centre of London, where they would be reunited with their families, with as much haste as possible. Statements from them being deferred for a few days at least, in view of the ordeal they had suffered.

After the young ladies had been escorted away, Holmes and I were briefly left alone and Holmes pointed out the bricked up windows, which he had observed from outside the previous night. Ventilation shafts had been provided in lieu of the windows, and it was by spending some time listening at the external openings to these, that he had gleaned the information he had sought.

Holmes then found a lantern, and we went outside to examine a large out-building, which Holmes had noticed the night before, but had not the means to explore at that time. It was not locked and, when we got inside, we found that it was a warehouse, full of boxes of stationery, great rolls of paper and the like. There were not a few typewriters, still in their boxes, new and unused. In one corner was an old-fashioned printing press, of German manufacture, covered with a dust-sheet.

We then went back to the study to find Lestrade. Holmes took the opportunity to type out a few sentences on each typewriter in the room. For comparison purposes, I assumed.

In one of the drawers of the desk we found several astronomical charts, a bar of gold sealing-wax together with the lightning-sceptre seal, and notes that Lassinger intended to take the lives of the abducted women, followed by his wife, his two daughters, and finally, after setting fire to the house to create what he described as a pagan funeral pyre, himself. His reasons for contemplating these obscene acts were complex and beyond normal human understanding. They testified to Lassinger's

"First of all, I must tell you that I am but recently widowed," she said. "Tom, my husband of more than thirty years, died five weeks ago, and it is from this that my difficulties began. When Tom was a young man, he was a surveyor, working for the Mexican government in the north of the country. While he was there, the territory was ceded to the United States to become what is now California."

"That happened in February, 1848," said my friend.

"Yes, sir, that was the year, and he was living near Sacramento, which at that time had only a handful of inhabitants. Be that as it may, he was in the area which later became the focus of the great gold rush of '49, and, due to his proximity, he was one of the first to stake his claim - I believe that was the term used. He was very lucky, and found a considerable deposit. He stayed there until it was all worked out, and then he made his way to San Francisco, arriving there in the summer of 1850. It was his intention to take ship, and sail back to England via the Pacific route. When he got to San Francisco, however, he found the port and town in utter chaos. The port was jammed with hundreds of ships, which had been abandoned by the sailors who had joined the rush to the foothills, and so he was obliged to remain in San Francisco for months, before he could get a ship. While he was there, he had many adventures. On more than one occasion, he had to resort to violence to protect his gold, which was in the form of dust and nuggets. He had more than a hundred bags of it, worth about £200,000 sterling. It was this time in San Francisco which made him reluctant to let the gold out of his sight. It became an obsession of his, to remain with him all his life, as you will hear. Anyway, after a long sea-voyage, via China and the Cape of Good Hope, where the ship almost foundered in a terrible storm, he arrived back in England in late 1851. Soon after he arrived, he bought land in Kent, near Sevenoaks, built

127

a fine house, which he called Sacramento House, and settled down to the life of a country squire. Not long after this, I met and married him."

Here the lady began to weep, dabbing her eyes with a lace handkerchief. Holmes offered her a glass of brandy, which she declined, declaring that she never touched alcohol of any kind. She consented to take coffee instead and, after this had been brought and she had drunk a cup, she seemed to recover herself.

I had expected, when she began her narrative, that my friend would show his usual impatience, but, to my surprise, he sat quietly listening, as if spellbound.

"And now I come to the reason I have come to consult you, Mr. Holmes," she went on, when she was fully recovered, "it is difficult for me to speak of it, for fear that you might think that I value money more than I valued my husband. I can assure you that such is not, and never has been the case. I loved my husband dearly. As I have said, my husband was reluctant, due to his difficulties in America, to let his gold out of his sight and to my consternation, when first I took up residence in Sacramento House, I found that he insisted on keeping the gold hidden in a specially made secret strongbox, in the wall of our bedroom. Even then, he checked that it was still there several times a day, and kept a revolver about him at all times.

"Despite my protests, he would not deposit the gold in a bank, preferring, once a year, to take some of it up to town to sell in order to cover household expenses. In the end, whether because of my protests, or because he could hardly bear to leave the house for any reason, even to sell a portion of his gold, he removed it to a place which he kept secret from everybody, including myself. He did indicate, however, that the hiding place was within the confines of the estate, but gave no details. It did cross my mind, on hearing this, that in the event of his sudden demise, a very difficult situation would arise. I did not raise the subject at that time, but I made up my mind to broach it, if he ever became ill or infirm. This never happened, because he was fit and strong up to the moment of his death and he died so suddenly, so very suddenly."

Here the poor woman began to weep, once more. Holmes rose to his feet, placed his hand on her shoulder, and said, "I understand the situation perfectly. Please try not to be so upset. I shall do all in my power to help you find the gold, and I am certain I shall not fail."

The lady looked up into his eyes, and briefly rested her hand on his. She smiled wanly up at him and dried her eyes. When he was quite certain that she was reassured, Holmes resumed his seat.

"Tell me," he said, "If you can bear to speak of it, how, exactly, did he die?"

The lady cleared her throat, and began to speak again. "We had had some old friends to dinner. After the meal, I chatted to the wife, while Tom withdrew to the billiard room with the husband. During the game, he had some kind of stroke, collapsed, and was dead within a few minutes. He, who never had a day's illness in his life, not even a headache."

Again she raised the handkerchief to her eyes, and again we had to allow a decent interval to elapse before she sufficiently recovered.

"Did he say anything before he died?" enquired my friend.

"I was alone with him at the last, and all he said was 'The study. The four walls.' I am not absolutely sure whether he said 'The four walls', or 'The four ways', his voice was very weak at that time. I am certain that he said 'The study'. However, there is a coaching inn named *The Four Ways*, about three miles from where we live."

"Did he have much to do with the inn?"

"Very little, he probably only went there half a dozen times, perhaps, during the whole time we lived at Sacramento House."

"I suppose you have made a search of the study?"

"Indeed I have. In fact, helped by my daughter I have searched the entire house, including all books and papers."

"And found no clue as to the whereabouts of the gold?"

"None whatsoever."

"Have you made representations at the coaching inn?"

"Yes, but the landlord knows nothing of these matters, or, at least, says that he knows nothing."

"Hum! this is a pretty little problem."

"It is not a little thing to me and my daughter," said the lady, bridling a little.

"I am so sorry, I assure you that I did not intend to make light of this matter, it was no more than a turn of phrase."

The lady seemed mollified by this declaration.

"Do you have many servants?" Holmes enquired.

"We have eight, four who work in the grounds, and four in the house." She seemed surprised at the question.

"Have any of them left, since your husband's death?"

"No, they are all present, as ever."

"Is there anyone in the neighbourhood, who suddenly seems to be well-off, since your husband died?"

"Not to my knowledge?" She still seemed to be puzzled.

"You must forgive these last questions. I was only trying to determine whether or not the gold might have fallen into the wrong hands. I think we can assume, from your answers, that it has not."

"You have said, have you not, that your husband was obsessed with the safety of his gold?"

"Yes that is so."

"Was there, then, a part of the house or grounds, which he seemed to visit, or frequent, more than any other?"

"He spent a great deal of time in his study and he was very fond, in fine weather, of sitting on the terrace at the front of the house, and looking at the view through his telescope. Other than those places, he seemed to have no particular preferences. Years ago, when photography was a hobby of his, he used to spend a lot of time in his darkroom, a room off the study. He was very fond of taking photographs of the house and grounds, which he would then develop in his darkroom. He had many of these photographs framed, and had them hung in various parts of the house."

"You say that his hobby of photography was prevalent years ago, I take it, then, that he has not followed it for some time?"

"Not for about the last ten years."

"Thank you for your frank and open account, I shall be pleased to take your case. I think I have heard all that I need, for now. When may my colleague and myself come down to your house in Kent?"

"Now that I have seen you, I shall travel back this evening. You would be very welcome, if you came to-morrow."

"We shall see you to-morrow then. Would you excuse me for a moment?"

"Most certainly."

Holmes rose to his feet, and took down a copy of *Bradshaw*. After leafing through it for a few moments, he came to the relevant page.

"There is a train from London, which arrives at Sevenoaks at ten-twenty," he said, looking up at her.

"That would be very convenient. I shall send our coachman to meet you." Our visitor rose, I rose also, and, after Holmes had briefly clasped her hand, we wished her a good-day.

When she had gone, Holmes and I returned to our chairs beside the fire, Holmes knocked out his pipe on the grate, refilled it, and sat with his eyes closed, his hands folded behind

131

his head. Gradually, he became wreathed in smoke. I knew better than to disturb his train of thought, and, gingerly, so as not to make a noise, I took up the newspaper again. I had read perhaps two pages, when Holmes spoke.

"So, Watson, a curious tale."

"Very curious," said I, relinquishing the paper. "Do you think that you will be able to help her?" I went on.

"You mean: do I think that I will be able to find the missing gold?"

"I suppose so."

"What one man can hide, another can surely find."

I waited for him to elaborate, but he did not.

"Did you notice, Holmes, how unhappy she was to talk about money at this time of her bereavement?"

"Yes. I felt for her, it is an awkward predicament for her."

Conversation languished after these exchanges, and I took up the paper for the third time that day.

The next morning was fine and dry, and unseasonably warm for October. We entrained at Charing Cross, and were soon rattling through the Kent countryside. The journey was a short one, and in less than no time, it seemed, we had pulled up at Sevenoaks station.

There was not a breath of wind, and the sun slanted through the smoke and steam of our arrival, which hung over the station, as if reluctant to leave. In the distance, I could see some trees clothed in russet. A few leaves in the station yard bore testimony to the fact that winter was not far away.

A man, dressed in a greatcoat and curiously shaped hat, approached us, touched his forehead, and enquired whether we were Sherlock Holmes and friend. On being told that we were, he took our bags, and led the way to a smart, black carriage and pair. Once we were ensconced, and had started off, I reflected on the curious power that all good coachmen had: that of distinguishing, from perhaps many others, which person, or persons, they had been sent to meet.

We must have been driving for four or five miles, more or less to the south, because the sun was before us the whole time, when we reached a pair of gates, beyond which lay a wood. We drove through the gates and, at length, reached a fork in the road. The driver took the left-hand turning, and, soon afterwards, we reached the edge of a considerable clearing in the trees, where some horses grazed. At this point, the road curved away to the left and right, around the boundary fence at the edge of the clearing.

A large house stood near the top of the clearing, directly opposite us, overlooking a slight downward slope. Between us and the house, in the middle of the clearing, stood a plinth built of stone, surmounted by an obelisk of the same material. The coachman took the left curve.

The house, rectangular in plan and of three storeys, had castellated walls. The roof could just be seen through the castellation, which were set in an unbroken line in front of it. Set on the three corners within view, were castellated turrets, with inverted, conical bottoms. In the centre of each turret was a flagpole, although no flags were to be seen. I assumed that there was a fourth turret, on the corner which was out of sight. In front of the house was a terrace, upon which were a number of pieces of statuary. The front of the terrace was contained by a wall, surmounted by a stone balustrade, pierced in the centre, and at that point a stone stairway led down to the clearing.

The road ran behind the house, and we came to rest at the main entrance. Standing on the steps were the lady of yesterday and a young woman, whom I assumed was her daughter. I nudged Holmes, who had lain back on his seat, with his eyes closed, as if asleep, for the whole of the journey from the station, and he looked about him.

We descended from the carriage and were greeted by the older woman. She introduced her companion, who proved to be her daughter, to us. The widow ushered us into a long, pleasant drawing-room, which evidently ran from the front of the house to the back. The windows at one end gave a fine view of the open space at the front of the house. A cheery log-fire burned in the large fireplace, and, after I had admired the view, I stood there warming my back. Holmes, meanwhile, had seated himself in an armchair near the fire, and was holding out his hands to the blaze.

"We have started to burn wood," said the widow, "in case..." her words tailed off.

"Don't worry, mamma," said her daughter, whose name was Catherine, "I am sure that Mr. Sherlock Holmes and his friend will be able to find dadda's gold." As she said this, she, gave Holmes, and then myself, sweet smiles, which were full of hope.

I found myself thinking that the faith which Miss Catherine had in our abilities was touching, and I prayed that all would be well. We sat there for a time, talking about trivial matters. I noticed, that now the subject of the gold had been broached, it was the one thing which was not discussed. It was almost painfully avoided by both mother and daughter, as if further talk of it would break some kind of spell.

After a time a woman knocked and announced that luncheon was ready, accordingly we all followed her into the dining room. When we had finished our luncheon, the widow told Holmes, and myself, that we were free to go anywhere in the house and grounds in the pursuit of our quest, and that she and her daughter would be in the small sitting room, if by any chance we required either of them.

"Thank you," said my friend, "I think we shall begin in the study, if you would be kind enough to show us where it is." We were escorted to the study, and the two women withdrew.

"You will recall, Watson," said Holmes, when we were alone, "that the dying man's last words were: 'The study. The four walls.' It is possible that the latter phrase was 'The four ways', but we will discount that for now. We will assume that the landlord of that establishment knows nothing of this matter."

The walls of the study were covered by a green paper of sombre tone. There were eight framed photographs of the front of the house, two on each wall, taken from different angles, and from some distance away. The walls were otherwise bare.

Holmes carefully removed the photographs, one by one, stacking them, equally carefully, on the floor under the desk. He then minutely examined the walls with a lens, occasionally moving a piece of furniture out in order to so. Then he sounded every square inch of the walls with his knuckles. While he was doing this, I looked out of the window. The study was on the second floor, and seemed to be in the centre of the front of the house. I could see the whole of the clearing, which now appeared to be roughly circular in shape. The obelisk, which I had noted earlier, was now directly in front of me.

I turned back to the room, Holmes had finished his examination of the walls, which must have yielded nothing, and was examining the backs of the photographs.

"It is regrettable," said he, "but I think that I will have to cut open the paper at the backs of all these photographs, in order to see whether anything is concealed within them. Would you be so good as to ask permission from the widow to do so?"

I left the room, and after making enquiries of one of the servants, found the small sitting room.

"Mr. Holmes must do anything he thinks fitting," replied the widow, when I had put his question to her.

We had a merry time of it, Holmes and I, sitting on the floor, carefully slitting the paper at the backs of all the photographs, and examining the contents. I, for one, felt like a guilty schoolboy. At the end of this session of vandalism, we had found nothing, and were no further forward than before.

"What about the photographs hanging in other parts of the house?" I hazarded.

"I think, Watson, that we will leave this line of enquiry for the present and turn our attention to something else."

Holmes rose and went to the darkroom. It had been painted on the inside with black paint, and we were obliged to throw a window open to get enough light to see the interior, which was sparsely furnished. There were a number of cameras - one quite large - tripods, developing dishes, chemicals and other paraphernalia associated with photography.

Everything was very neat, but a layer of dust showed that the room had not been used for some time. There was nothing of any interest, except a stack of glass negatives, stored in thick, brown envelopes. These proved to be the negatives of the photographs, whose mountings we had so recently damaged, together with some others. A large, brass telescope, on a tripod, stood just behind the door.

Holmes declared that he had to obtain a map featuring the house and grounds - if necessary, he would send to Town for one. We went to the small sitting room to appraise the widow of Holmes's intention.

"There is no need to send to London for a such a map," the widow told us. "When all building work had been finished and the grounds had been laid out, my husband made two fine maps of the estate, and he showed them to me. He was, after all, a surveyor by profession. Whenever an addition of any kind was made, he took pleasure in setting it in its proper place on both maps, together with the date of its completion."

"Where are they to be found?" enquired Holmes.

"Catherine, my dear, would you please show the two gentlemen your father's map-room."

The map-room proved to be a small, dusty room at the back of the house. One wall was fitted with a set of deep shelves, which had been divided up into square pigeon-holes. Most of these were filled with rolled charts and maps, the others lay empty. In the corner, were two battered tubular cases, held fast with frayed leather straps, which probably held tripods for the two theodolites which we found, in their cases, on a shelf. There were also a few picks, shovels, and other tools, together with a quantity of rope and pulley blocks.

After the girl had gone, we turned our attention to the rolled maps in the pigeon-holes. Luckily, the pigeon-holes were labelled, and we soon found the roll to which the widow had referred. When we came to unroll it, however, only one map was to be found. Holmes wrinkled his forehead a little at this discovery, and carefully looked over the other pigeon-holes, but without success. He shrugged his shoulders, dusted off the drawing-board with a piece of cloth, and spread the map upon it, holding it at the corners with clips which we found there.

The map, of large scale, showed the entire estate of the late Mr. Hanley. We could see that the clearing, in which lay the house, was almost perfectly circular, the house being in the north, near the perimeter.

"Hanley was obviously a very methodical man," observed Holmes. "You can see that the stone obelisk is at the centre of this circular clearing, and the date of its completion, July, 1852, shows that it was built at the same time as the house itself, which bears the dates: June, 1852, and May, 1853. They must be, respectively, the date when work began on the house, and the date of its completion."

"What can we learn from this, Holmes?" I enquired.

"Not a very great deal, I am afraid," said my friend, "except that the gold is unlikely to be hidden in the foundations of the obelisk."

"Why is one of the two maps of the estate missing, do you think?" I asked.

"I am unsure, but I think it likely that the missing map holds clues to the whereabouts of the gold, and that, in itself, is a clue. It means that the gold is probably not in the house, but is elsewhere, in the grounds. I think that the methodical, geometrical mind of Mr. Hanley, must have played a part in his choice of the place of concealment. We must not, nevertheless, narrow our field of search too much."

After we had pored over the map for some time, and after my friend had examined it carefully with a lens, for traces of erasures, impressions caused by something written on paper, while resting on the map, of which there were none, we left the map-room to prepare for dinner. This meal was a solemn affair. We came down together, and when we entered the dining room, our hostess, and her daughter, looked at our faces, and finding no light of discovery in either of them, carefully avoided asking any questions about our progress.

After dinner, all four of us repaired to the long room into which we had been shown on arrival. The ladies occupied the time before retiring, with a few hands of some card game or other. Holmes and I sat either side of the fireplace, much as we would have done in Baker Street. The two ladies had given us permission to smoke our pipes.

The women addressed remarks to Holmes and to myself, but Holmes never made any reply and I was obliged to be our spokesman. He sat squarely in his armchair, with his eyes closed, puffing furiously at his pipe. From time to time, he would mutter something under his breath, and on one occasion, he sprang to his feet, the smoke from his pipe flowing down his back like a cloak, and paced wildly up and down before the fire.

Nothing of this was unfamiliar to me, but the effect upon the two ladies can easily be imagined. More than once, I saw them exchanging puzzled glances and, when my friend sprang to his feet, they stared at him in undisguised alarm. They looked to me for some sign that all was well, that my companion, despite all appearances, was not deranged. For my part, I sat as composedly as I could, trying to give the assurance that they obviously so badly needed, by preserving an outward calm.

It was not very long before the two ladies had had enough of Holmes's odd behaviour, and they retired for the night. I felt a profound relief at their departure, because preserving an appearance of equanimity had become rather trying, and when my friend came to himself once more, I suggested to him that we follow the suit of our hostesses.

"They have gone up then?" he said in a perplexed manner, looking around the room.

"Yes, Holmes," said I, as I took him gently by the arm, and led him out of the room, past a servant, who was obviously waiting to see to the lamps, and settle the fire for the night.

Early the next morning some sound, which I could not place, awakened me. A grey light filtered through the curtains, I listened carefully, but the noise was not repeated. It had had a strange booming quality, seeming to emanate from the wall behind my bed-head. I looked at my watch, it said seven-fifteen. I got up and donned a dressing gown. Then I heard the sound again, many times repeated. This time I soon realised that it came from somewhere far below me. I left my room, and went downstairs - the sounds were perceptibly louder.

By tracing the origin of the noise, I came to a door under the stairs, on the ground floor. When I opened it, I saw a flight of stairs leading down into the cellars, here the sounds were very loud. I reached the floor of the cellars, and, through a doorway, I could see a dim light. I made my way towards the light, and, in the thick dust which swirled around it, I could see a shadowy figure wielding a heavy hammer. It was Holmes, in his shirtsleeves, attacking one of the many stone-built pillars, which supported the floor above. On a small table near him, were two lamps. As I approached, there was a sudden, loud rumble, and a great mass of masonry fell to the floor, Holmes dropped the hammer, picked up one of the lamps, and peered into the large hole he had made in the pillar.

"Holmes!" I cried, "are you mad? What on earth are you doing, and at such an early hour?"

"Good morning, Watson," said Holmes, over his shoulder, "you are just in time - look at this."

I came up beside him, and looked into the hole. I could make out the angular shape of a large, metal box.

"Stand back, Watson, if you love me!"

He was obviously, for him, in a state of high excitement. He replaced the lamp beside its fellow on the table. I stood back, and watched, as a few more strokes of the hammer dislodged the box, which fell to the floor with a terrific crash and clatter, trailing a stout rope, tied to a large ring welded to its upper side. No sooner had this occurred, when Holmes pushed the box over with his foot, setting it so that its door was uppermost. He then redoubled his efforts with the hammer, this time at the door of the box, and smashed it in. He threw down the hammer, picked up the lamp once more, fell to his knees, and examined the contents by the light of the lamp. I noticed that the hand which held the lamp was trembling.

The box contained two bags of gold. One was full, the other almost empty. Holmes looked at me, his dust-streaked face a study of disappointment. My heart went out to him. He took the almost empty bag, opened it, and I caught the sparkle in the light of the lamp of a mass of golden particles.

Holmes rose, brushing the dust from his clothes. He seemed to have recovered his composure in the time it took to perform these actions, and he regarded me calmly.

"Well at least I have found some of the gold," said he, placing the lamp upon the floor.

"How on earth did you know that there was something hidden in that pillar?" I asked.

Holmes sat down on the small table, moving the other lamp to the floor to do so. He cleared his throat and seemed prepared to digress at some length, when we were interrupted by the arrival of the two ladies, and he got to his feet.

"Mr. Holmes!" said the elder lady, "you are in a very dusty and dishevelled state, you really must have a bath!" She did not seem at all put out by the sight of so much destruction.

"I fully intend to wash as soon as possible, ma'am," said my friend, "but first, please be so good as to look at these." He indicated the bags.

Both women stared at them, and the elder of them took up the bag which Holmes had opened. Her hand went up to her throat, and she looked upon my companion with eyes which sparkled in the light, like the particles of gold.

"I have not seen these bags for many years," she said. "I must confess that Catherine and I expressed our doubts about you, after we had retired for the night, but now I see that you are a clever man, whose great reputation is deserved. You may not have found the main hoard, but you are obviously hot on the trail. Tell me, how did you divine that this box was hidden in that pillar?"

"I will gladly tell everybody everything at breakfast," said Holmes.

Accordingly we four went back upstairs. I carried the bags of gold and deposited them, at Mrs. Hanley's request, in a cupboard in the long sitting room. We arranged to meet again, in the dining room, at eight-thirty.

The atmosphere at breakfast was very different from that prevailing at dinner the previous evening: there were smiles and happy faces. Holmes however was a little downcast, despite his discovery, and I could tell that the business of finding the bulk of the gold was pressing upon him, once again. It also occurred to me, that he was thinking that there might not be any more gold to be found. This idea, however, was obviously far from the minds of the two ladies.

When we had all finished, Holmes told us all how he lighted upon the pillar in the cellar, as a possible hiding place.

"First of all, I found that I could not sleep very well last night. My mind was filled with the theories which I had envisioned during the day, and, of course, at that hour, I could not test any of them. Eventually, I fell into a doze, and when I awoke, it was six, and as I lay there, it occurred to me that although I had been in every room in the house, I had not yet seen the cellar. I dressed, went downstairs, and found the cellar door without any difficulty. I then took possession of two lamps, and went down the stairs. I was there for quite some time, exploring. As you know, the cellar is divided into several rooms: the exact number is six, one of which holds coals. I started to sound the walls, with a large coal-hammer, but soon had to desist for fear of disturbing the household. I seated myself, to rest for a while, on an old chair in one corner of the largest cellar room, and, after a time, I started to idly count the many pillars, which supported the beams of the ground floor. The number I arrived at was fifteen: an odd number.

"I looked again, and I saw that although each supported beam was held by a pair of pillars, one beam, near the centre, had three, and, moreover, the centre pillar was built in a very different way. Instead of holding up a beam, it continued up between two beams, to the floorboards above. Because of this it was also a good deal bigger than the others. It had obviously been added after the house was completed, because the configuration of the pillars on either side was the same as that of all the others in the cellar. That is, they were the same distance apart, and each was the same distance from the corresponding wall.

"I found a small table, nearby, and drew it up to this supernumerary pillar. I stood upon it and, holding up a lamp, I peered into a crack, about half an inch in breadth, between the top of the pillar and the boards above. There was also a small space between the beams and the top of the pillar. The pillar was hollow, and I caught a glimpse of a rope hanging down inside. The presence of the cracks meant that the pillar was not, in fact, supporting anything.

"Clearly then, somewhere above, there was a trapdoor which communicated with this pillar. I could have found it by a system of careful measuring, but I threw caution to the winds, and after jumping down, and placing the lamps upon the table, I started to attack the pillar, with the hammer, at a point about half-way between the floor of the cellar, and the boards of the room above. It was not long after that, that Watson joined me, and you, yourselves, witnessed the rest."

A silence fell, and then the two ladies, and I, gave a little round of applause, during which Holmes's face flushed with a mixture of pleasure and embarrassment.

"I cannot quite comprehend how the trapdoor and pillar was used." I said, when all was calm again.

Holmes gave me a keen glance. "It is simple enough. The trap-door, in the floor of the room above, was thrown open, and the metal box was raised by means of the rope. Once it was in the room, the box could be opened, and some of the gold removed. Afterwards, it was lowered back down inside the hollow pillar by the same rope."

"What do you intend to do next, Mr. Holmes?" enquired Catherine, whose admiration was obviously fully restored.

"I propose to go to the study, for I believe that there must be something there which I have not seen. The dying man's words must have had some hidden meaning."

Holmes and I went to the study, and he gathered together the photographs, which had, until recently, adorned the walls, placed them on the desk, and fell to studying them minutely. He quickly became oblivious to my presence, and since I did not want to disturb his train of thought, I decided to take a walk around the clearing at the front of the house.

I set off, it was a lovely day, and as I walked slowly down the road by which we had reached the house, I could now see that it formed a complete circle around the clearing, just outside the perimeter fence, and that the curved road, from the main gates, joined it at a point almost exactly opposite the house, as a stalk joins an apple.

I had reached this point, and was leaning on the fence, smoking an after-breakfast pipe, and watching the horses, when I became aware of someone shouting. The sound came from the direction of the house - it was faint, but I recognised it as Holmes's voice. I looked up at the house, narrowing my eyes as I did so, and I could just make out Holmes's upper body, leaning out of what must be the window of the study, he was gesticulating with his arm. I understood that he had discovered something, and I set off back to the house, at a brisk trot.

When I got back to the house, I ran, panting, up the stairs to the study, Holmes stood at the threshold. I leaned over, with my hands on my knees, in order to catch my breath. During this time, Holmes was trying to tell me something about the photographs, but my condition made it very difficult to follow what he was saying. At length, I recovered somewhat and was able to turn my attention to my friend. He had arranged the photographs on the desk, in two rows of four, one row above the other.

"Look at these, Watson, and tell me what you see," said he.

I looked, but I could not really see anything of interest, save that Holmes had arranged them so that each photograph in the top row, had an almost identical photograph below it.

The field of view, in both cases, was identical, but it was obvious that the ones in the top row had been taken from a slightly higher standpoint. This could be most plainly seen from the point of view of the statuary on the terrace, at the front of the house. In the top row of photographs, the statuary stood a little lower against the walls of the house.

"I am afraid that I see nothing very remarkable about these photographs," I said, after a minute or two of studying them in silence.

"You can see just as much as I can," said Holmes, "but you infer nothing, whereas I infer a very great deal."

"What can you possibly infer from a set of views such as these?" I asked, only just keeping the heat out of my voice."

"In the first place, all four photographs of the bottom row have been taken at four different places, and their fellows, above, have been taken at the same places, but it is obvious that they have been taken at higher points."

"I can see that much." I replied.

"You will, I know, agree with me, that if we were to take the photographs, from the bottom row, down to the clearing at the front of the house, we would be able, after a little juggling about, to find the exact place where the photographer, Hanley, stood in each case, by comparing our view of the house, at that spot, with that depicted in each photograph?"

"Yes, I follow you that far, but would it help us to do so?"

Holmes ignored my question, and went on: "we could then find out how, or rather, why, the upper set of photographs were taken at a different, somewhat higher, place."

"Perhaps they were taken at the top of a ladder of some sort," I hazarded.

"Does it not occur to you, that they were, almost certainly, taken at a point some way up a convenient tree? And what is more, that each similar pair points to a specific tree?"

At last light began to dawn in my mind. "You mean that Hanley used these photographs to indicate certain trees, in the forestry around the clearing, trees which might, in their upper branches, hold clues of some kind?"

Holmes smiled at me, "Exactly so."

"Well then, we must take these photographs, and find those four trees." The excitement in my voice must have showed, because Holmes smiled at me again, putting his hand on my shoulder as he did so. He then gathered up the photographs, and swept out of the room. Without hesitation, I followed him.

Holmes set a fast pace, almost a run, and I had a hard time keeping up with him. We passed the two ladies, near the main entrance of the house: they spoke to us, but we did not stop to speak to them. As I went around the corner of the house, I looked back, and saw them standing together on the steps, open-mouthed with surprise. We soon reached a point in the road, almost directly opposite the front of the house, very close to where I had been standing when Holmes called to me from the study window.

We could easily see that two pairs of photographs had been taken at points to the left of this spot, while the other two pairs had been taken from points to the right. Holmes carefully placed the photographs on a grass verge, next to the perimeter fence, he then selected the one which had been taken at the extreme left, at the lower viewpoint, and by dint of comparing it with what we could see, we soon found ourselves standing on the exact spot where the photograph had been originally taken.

Immediately behind us, so that our backs were almost up against it, stood a large, sycamore tree. Holmes looked at me and then, more significantly, at the tree. He then ran back and fetched the photograph which had been taken at that spot, but from the higher viewpoint. Holding this photograph, he began to climb up the tree, comparing views as he did so.

"Be careful, Holmes," I called, as he began his ascent, but he did not take any notice, and was soon lost in the tangle of branches, from which most of the leaves had fallen. Hardly any time passed before I heard a delighted exclamation from my friend, who was, by now, some fifteen or twenty feet above me.

"What have you found?" I shouted. There was no answer, but I heard a scrambling noise, and dust and small debris started to fall around me. Holmes soon came back into view, and he jumped down at my feet, his face red with the exertion.

"Write this down, Watson," said he, panting a little, tossing the photograph on to the grass, and handing me a stub of pencil, and a small note book. "37 degrees," was all that he said.

I confess that I felt disappointed, as I wrote down the angle measurement, but his eyes were shining, and I surmised that this cryptic angle value had some deep meaning for him.

"How did you arrive at this..?" I began.

Holmes interrupted me. "At the point up the tree where the views coincided, I found a small copper plaque. It was nailed there, with copper nails, just above a branch, and therefore invisible from the ground. On it was inscribed the figure I have just given to you, together with the symbol indicating degrees."

"What does it mean?"

"I have no time to explain now," he said, still a little out of breath, "all will become clear later."

We found the other tree on the left, somewhat further from the house, and again he climbed up, returned, and gave me a figure to write down. This time, it was 48 degrees.

We then turned our attention to the two trees on the right. The one on the extreme right, bore the figure 33 degrees, and the one furthest from the house yielded the figure 51 degrees.

147

All the trees proved to be sycamores, set asymmetrically, on the other side of the road from the clearing, and in its lower half.

I was still mystified, but felt gratified that Holmes's speculation about the trees, and that my suggestion about clues in their upper branches, had borne fruit.

We gathered up the photographs, and made our way back to the house. During our manoeuvres, I had glanced up at the house, and had seen the two ladies standing on the terrace, watching us, and they met us as we came around to the main entrance.

Holmes and I stopped when we reached them, he apologised for our brusque behaviour earlier, and when he explained that he had found some valuable clues, they were more than ready to forgive both of us.

We returned to the map-room, where Holmes lost no time in opening up one of the tubular cases, which we had noted on our previous visit, and which proved, indeed, to hold tripods for the theodolites.

When he had them both out, mounted the theodolites upon them, and had tested them to his satisfaction, he asked me to help him to carry the better of the two to the first tree we had encountered, that on the extreme left.

We set the theodolite at the foot of the tree and Holmes asked me to stand under the tree on the extreme right of the clearing. Before I left him, he asked me to give him the note-book, open at the page where I had written down the angular measurements. He also told me that when he raised his arm, I was to come to help him to set up the instrument where I had stood and so that I could stand at the spot where he now had the theodolite. In other words, we were to change places.

I walked to the tree indicated, still completely in the dark as to what all this activity was about. In the distance, I could see him taking a sight through the theodolite in my direction, then the sun flashed on the lens of the instrument, as he turned it towards the house.

I saw him change the angle of elevation of the instrument, and, a few minutes later, he raised his arm, and I walked towards him. When we had changed places, again I saw him take a sight on me, then turn the instrument so that it pointed towards the house.

This procedure was repeated with the remaining two trees. When all this had been accomplished, I felt a little hot and bothered. When we met again I demanded to know what it was that we had been doing.

"In a word, my dear friend, triangulation," said he, with his eyes shining.

"Have you found out what it was that you wanted to know?"

"In every conceivable way. Those angular measurements, refer to the base angles of two triangles, and by setting the turning circles on the theodolites, to the smaller base angles first, and then, at the other two trees, to the two larger angles, the two triangles emerged, both of which had their apices at a point on the terrace of the house. I had to change the elevation of the instrument, in all four cases, and memorise what I saw, in order to find the common apex point of both triangles."

"What point, exactly?"

"I am going there now, and I am sure that you will accompany me."

"I do not understand why there were two triangles, when one would have served just as well."

"I rather think that Hanley was taking no chances. Trees, for instance, can suffer diseases, or otherwise decay. He wanted to ensure that there was more than one chance to unravel his secret."

"The secret of the hidden gold?"

"I believe so."

"Could not the triangles have been interpreted, so that their apexes coincided at some point to the south, away from the house?"

"No. The fact that the two trees bearing the smaller angles were nearer the house than those with the larger angles, meant that if their apexes were to coincide, the shallower triangle had to be above the deeper and not the other way around. This was, clearly, another reason for having two triangles."

Here, Holmes drew a circle in the dust of the road: inside it, he put a shallow triangle, so that its apex was a little distance below the top of the circle. He then drew a deeper, or taller triangle, so that the two apexes coincided. The base line of the deeper triangle was some distance below that of the shallower triangle.

"It is clear to me now," I exclaimed.

We walked back to the house, carrying the theodolite. On arrival, Holmes insisted that we put the instrument back into its container in the map-room. It was as if he wanted to put off the moment of truth about the place on the terrace, in case it should prove to be a dead end.

We went to the terrace and the two ladies followed. Holmes walked up to a large statue of Britannia seated upon her throne. The statue was some six feet tall and stood towards the front of the terrace, just before the stone staircase leading to the clearing. It was flanked either side by a number of other, smaller, statues.

"This statue was shown by our work, to be at the apex of both triangles," said he, placing his hand upon it. "Therefore the gold has to be hidden inside it or, possibly, under it, unless I have deceived myself."

He turned to the elder of the two ladies, and I could see anxiety etched upon his features. "Tell me - when was this statue acquired?"

"All the statues have been here for at least five and twenty years."

Holmes features relaxed to bear signs of relief. "That bodes well. Now we are faced with the task of moving it, or, at least, we must tilt it on its side. Fortunately, it has a square base, which will help us."

Holmes fell to his knees at the foot of the statue, and carefully examined each side of the base, where it met the floor of the terrace. He straightened up, brushing the knees of his trousers and I caught a gleam in his eye. "The bottom edge of one side of the base is a little rounded, and the stone next to it shows slight signs of wear," he declared. "It has been tilted in that direction before - in all probability, a number of times."

"But," I expostulated, "how on earth could the one man who knew the secret of this statue, have tilted it, in the manner you describe? It must, at the very least, weigh about two tons."

Holmes turned to me, and smiled. "By means of a block and tackle."

"The block and tackle in the map-room!"

The items were soon procured and set up. One end was secured to a pillar of the stone balustrade, the other was fastened around the neck of the figure.

Holmes and I worked at the block and tackle, and the statue began to tilt. The effort we needed to use was surprisingly small, considering the great weight with which we were dealing.

"We must be very careful," cautioned my friend, "we do not want to tilt it too far, and have it crash to the floor of the terrace. I am certain that Hanley knew exactly what he was about. When he did this, luckily, the centre of gravity of the statue is low, and we should be able to tilt it quite far, without any danger."

When Holmes was quite certain that we could tilt it no further, we tied the end of the rope we had been pulling to the balustrade, and went to examine the area which, until recently, had been covered by the base of the statue. During the whole of the time that we had grappled with it, the two ladies had stood well back. Now they came forward, as my friend went upon his knees at its base once more.

I heard him give a cry of satisfaction and, peering into the angle made by the base of the statue and the terrace, I could see, set a little below the level of the terrace floor, a square flagstone with a rusty, iron ring in its centre.

Holmes and I struggled with this for a time, then it yielded, and we gazed into a shaft, about two feet square. The shaft was lined with lead sheet, and an iron ladder was affixed to one side. Lamps were brought, and Holmes climbed down the ladder. After a few moments, I heard him call my name and I went down the ladder to join him.

I found myself in a small room, not more than five feet square, and about six feet deep. Piled to the sides of the room were dozens of canvas bags, and more were underfoot. We had found the gold. We climbed out of that place each carrying a bag. The two ladies were overjoyed at the sight, and even more overjoyed, when they heard that there were many more bags below.

After we had been effusively thanked, Holmes and I took the carriage into Sevenoaks, the statue being temporarily replaced. Holmes made arrangements, by wire, with a London bank, to come and collect all the gold. This was to take place upon the morrow. At the two ladies' request, we agreed to stay until the gold was collected, and, that evening, they gave a grand dinner in our honour.

After the meal, we all retired to the long drawing room, and much praise was lavished upon us. At one point, Mrs. Hanley went to the cupboard where the find of yesterday had been stored and approached my friend, carrying the full bag of gold.

"Mr. Holmes, I want you to have this as a reward for the wonderful service you have undertaken, on behalf of myself and my daughter."

There was an awkward pause, but, seeing that to refuse would cause offence, my friend smiled, nodded, and accepted his reward. Catherine asked Holmes why there had been two hiding places.

"The reason there were two hiding places, was one of convenience. It would have been irksome to move that statue every time some gold was needed. Your late father conceived the idea of the secondary hiding place, in the stone pillar, so that when the statue was moved, enough gold could be brought up to suffice for two or three years."

"But," the girl went on, "when did dadda construct the hiding places? I know that he could not have done so when mamma and I were staying in the house."

"I think I can answer that," said her mother. "You must remember that every year he would send us on a holiday abroad, and then would join us later, perhaps after two weeks. During those same two weeks, all the servants would take their annual holiday. He would have his holiday with us, after they came back."

"And I suppose the hiding place, under the statue, was one which could be checked on every day," I mused. "He could see the statue from his study. It explains why the study and the terrace were his two favourite places."

Holmes and the two ladies nodded.

The next day two bank officials arrived to weigh the gold in the presence of all four of us and issue a preliminary receipt. They explained that the total value of the consignment would not be known until all the gold had been assayed.

After they had gone, Holmes and I bade farewell to the two ladies, and we left for London.

That evening, in Baker Street, Holmes opened the bag which he had accepted from Mrs. Hanley. We gazed at the gold it contained for some time, without speaking.

"What will you do with it?" I enquired.

Holmes gave a short laugh. "I will have it valued, and, after selling it, I will keep the money in a separate deposit account for my eventual retirement."

"I pray that that day will be long in coming," I said fervently, "and I am sure that those two ladies would agree with me."